City of Kaus
REBELLION

BOOK 5

DANI HOOTS

"Destiny is a funny thing. You never know how things are going to work out. But if you keep an open mind and an open heart, I promise you will find your own destiny someday."

—Uncle Iroh

CHAPTER I

Ellie

I watched as Zach left the infirmary. I had no words to explain why I had kept the truth from him. Perhaps because I hadn't wanted to believe it was true—perhaps I wanted to go back to how things were before the attack, so I ignored all the things he had done. All the things I had done.

Zach and I were far from innocent as well. We had killed to survive, just like Cor had. The only difference was that we didn't hunt our own kind.

Ghosts haunted us both, and I figured Cor was suffering as much as I was.

Turning to my brother and Mae, I found they were glaring at me.

My brother was the first to speak. "Ellie, tell us the truth. Tell us what you know."

I felt tears begin to run down my cheeks. I opened my mouth and closed it again. There were no words to describe what was going on.

Mae pinched the bridge of her nose. "I've had enough of this. For now, put the Sirian prince in a cell and take Ellie back to her home and watch her. I will talk to the council and see how we should proceed."

Edmund nodded as he gestured to me. "Come on, Ellie. Let's go."

I nodded but not before taking a glance at Gabe. His eyes were wide as he stared at his hands. I couldn't blame him for what he was about to do. I would have done the same—we all would have. I would do everything I could to keep him safe. Even if it meant having to leave all this behind.

Especially since I had a feeling this all wasn't going to end well for any of us.

Edmund walked me back to my house without

saying a word. It was still nighttime, so no one else was out, which I was thankful for. I didn't want any eyes on me—not right now. Not with tears running down my face.

Since my hut was close to Edmund and Claude's, Claude was sitting on his porch, waiting for us. The moment we showed up, he stood and hurried to us.

"What happened?" he asked. "Are you all right? Why are you crying?"

I wiped the tears off my face. I knew this was going to happen when we saw the Kausian they'd brought in—I knew they were all going to find out the truth—but I hadn't taken into consideration they would find out that I'd known what he had done. We should have left with him—I should have left all this behind before they knew the truth. But I wanted a place to belong again. I wanted my home.

Edmund nodded to their hut. "Can you watch her while I look for Zach? I think he needs a minute, and I want to hear from him what is going on first."

Claude slowly nodded. "Yeah, I can do that..." He held out his arm. "Come on, Ellie. Let's go."

I didn't know what was worse—going to face Zach or the questions I knew Claude was going to ask. Once he knew the truth, would he still want to be with me? Who was I kidding? He deserved better than me.

We stepped inside their hut, and Claude pulled up a chair for me. "Here, sit. Do you need anything?"

I shook my head as I sat down. "No, I'm fine."

He took a seat across from me on the bed. He was quiet for a minute, waiting for me to say something.

I knew I should just tell him the truth since it was going to all come out soon anyway. But every time I wanted to confess, it felt as if something was in my throat.

"Is this about Cor?" Claude finally commented. "I noticed he was missing this evening."

I let out a laugh, not that any of this was funny. It was more of a laugh out of irony. "Somewhat."

"Did he make a run for it?"

I nodded. "He did."

"Typical of him. He could never commit to anything."

"That's not…" I let out a sigh. "It's a lot more complicated than that."

He leaned forward. "Then tell me what happened. I want to help, Ellie. Just let me help."

I glanced up at him. His eyes were genuine—

he'd always been genuine. He had always wanted to be there for me ever since we were kids. I rubbed my face.

"The Kausian that was brought back… he was used by Byron to kill the Sirian queen. He killed Gabe's mother."

Claude's eyes widened. "What?"

"And… Gabe tried to kill him."

Claude was silent.

"I can't blame him. He saw his mother assassinated in front of him. By someone wearing his own face." I whispered the last part.

Standing up, Claude rubbed his forehead. "This is not good."

I shook my head. "No, it's not. I can't blame him for wanting revenge. I would have done the same thing in his position."

"I agree. Problem is that the council isn't going to see it that way. They will see it as a threat and wonder if he is going to attack another Kausian and blame us all." He let out a sigh. "Now what does all this have to do with Cor leaving?"

I looked back down at my hands. "That… that's a long story."

"We have time."

I took a deep breath, not knowing what all I should tell him. I wasn't exaggerating when I said it was a long story. "I have so much blood on my hands, Claude. So much."

He knelt down beside me. "And that is okay. You did what you had to in order to survive. I understand that."

"How many men have you killed, Claude? How many men have you delivered to people, knowing full well that they were going to be tortured or killed? Knowing deep down that some of those people were innocent and were just in the wrong place at the wrong time? Or that they made one small mistake and pissed off the wrong people? How many have you murdered with your own hands in order to eat the next day?" I rubbed my face. "Zach and I tried to live in the wilderness— we really did. But then bandits came, and they tried to take it all away. They were the first…"

"Ellie, it doesn't matter anymore. You are safe. You are here."

I shook my head. "After everything that has happened, I really doubt that, Claude. They are going to blame us. They are going to hold us responsible for Gabe. And Cor…"

"What did he do, Ellie? Please tell me."

A voice came from the doorway. "He was the one who gave the codes to the Silurians."

I turned to find my brother there. He was frowning and watching me. I didn't know if he also blamed me for everything or if he was just watching my reaction. He stepped inside, and Zach followed him.

Claude turned back to me. "What?"

"It's not… That's not…"

Edmund raised his voice. "Then what happened, Ellie? Tell us, since you know more of what happened than anyone here."

I took a deep breath and let it out slowly. "It's all my fault. I wanted a better life… I wanted to leave Kaus. Cor knew that so he… he found a sponsor, or so he thought. He was being tutored. He was promised a spot at a university in the Human Zone. He trusted… But it was all for nothing. Byron was using him to get the codes.

"The Silurians ambushed him one day… He didn't know what would happen. They threatened me apparently. So he gave them the codes, thinking they would just… I don't know… just take over. Would being ruled by them be any worse than what our life was like? Or at least, that was what was going through his head. He never imagined they would attack."

Everyone stared at me, processing this information.

Claude rubbed his face. "You were protecting the man who brought the destruction of our kind."

"He was used by Byron. Byron wants all the nonhuman species dead. Or wanted… His family has been weaving an elaborate web for generations in order to create a world where only humans reign. If it wasn't Cor, he would have found another way in."

Edmund shook his head. "Stop making excuses for him, Ellie! Everyone is dead because of him!"

"What would you have done if it was me who gave the codes, Edmund?" I shot back. "He thought they had me—he thought they were going to kill me. All this happened because of me. He's not the only one responsible. He was trying to make a better life and was used. This is all Byron's fault and his family's. And he used us to take out the Silurians. We aren't innocent either."

Edmund frowned. "They had it coming."

"Yeah, well, a lot of people thought the same

about us. It was because of Byron's lineage that everyone hated us. We used to be revered. Did you know that? Only a couple of generations ago."

"Fine. Even if I buy into the destruction of our kind being because of Byron, you are leaving out an important bit—the part about Cor becoming a bounty hunter against our kind," Edmund added.

"What?" Claude turned to me. "He was hunting our kind?"

"I hunted people too. Am I a monster as well?"

Zach slammed his fist into the doorframe. "Quit the bullshit, Ellie! Was he or wasn't he hunting our kind?"

I stared at him. Zach never yelled like that—not unless he was extremely angry. I slowly nodded. "He did. For Krax, the Silurian who attacked Kaus. He wanted revenge, and it was the only way to get close."

"He could have killed him without doing all that," Zach exclaimed.

"He wanted to make him suffer. He wanted to be able to go into the Silurian Zone and kill everyone close to Krax before killing him slowly. Then Byron killed Krax, and it was all for nothing."

Everyone was silent.

"Do you still love him?" Claude asked. "After everything he has done and leaving you yet again, do you still love him?"

"I shouldn't. I should hate him, and I thought I did. But after finding him—after finding out the truth that it was for me—I just… I can't hate him. And it hurts so much."

Claude frowned as he stood up. "I need to take a walk." With that, he left us.

CHAPTER II

Zach

Ellie couldn't be serious.

After all this time, how could she still love him? She knew he had hurt our people, and she still cared about him. It was one thing to forgive him about the attack because she was right. He was tricked. He was trying to do good, and he could have never imagined what they would do to our people. But to hunt our people down for Krax so he could seek revenge… I couldn't even fathom it.

And yet she didn't care—she didn't care that he killed our people and was ordered to kill us. She still loved him. She still wanted to be with him even though he left her behind. More than once.

If I were Claude, I would give up on her.

"How could you be such a fool?" Edmund asked his sister before I could.

She shook her head. "I don't know, all right? I just love him. I always have, and I always will. We can't control our heart any more than we can control the suns."

Edmund ran his hand over his face. "If you had any morals, you would have given up on him long ago. You are just holding on to something that isn't there. You want to believe that after all this the two of you would live a happy life as if none of it has happened, but you know that isn't possible—you know he will never choose you first. He will always choose himself."

Ellie didn't respond to his comment but looked away.

"You know as well as I that you should have picked Claude a long time ago. I told you again and again that the two of you—"

"I am sorry, brother, that I didn't follow the step-by-step plan you had in place for me growing up. Sorry I made my own choices in life and didn't seek your approval for every single one of them," Ellie lashed out.

Great, they were having another sibling fight. I didn't miss having to witness their fights when we were younger. It wasn't often, but when they fought, they fought loud and hard. It made me thankful I was an only child—at least, in that aspect. They typically got along, and Ellie looked up to her brother and wanted to be like him, but she definitely did not go to him for romantic advice, and I think that always frustrated him.

"And maybe if you did listen to me, our whole home wouldn't have been destroyed!" Edmund exclaimed.

"Byron would have still attacked us one way or another! It wasn't Cor's fault!" Ellie countered.

"Maybe if that little shit actually had come to us with his problems instead of running off and moping, then we could have saved our home!"

"You know as well as I that there was nothing the Kausians could have done! They would have spun it as us attacking or something, and the entire world would have been against us more so than they already were!" Ellie yelled back.

I took a seat on the bed. This was going to be one of their longer squabbles. If I could take a nap with this noise going on, I would, but they were too loud.

"You are always defending him! Do you hear yourself? He left you! He left Zach! He has now even left his new boyfriend, which I might add means he moved on. Do you think he is going to leave him for you?"

"I never said I wanted him to leave Gabe."

"Oh, but I know you, Ellie. You want him to. You want to be the hero and help Cor so he will rely on you and want you in his life again. You are always trying to help him and save him, thinking he will end up with you. He is a loose cannon, Ellie, always was and always will be."

She shook her head. "That's not true—I don't always save him."

I started counting on my fingers how many times Ellie had gotten Cor out of trouble. Luckily, she had her back to me so she couldn't see what I was doing. I lost count after about 15 incidences, and that was just when we were still in school. Since these last few weeks, it had to have been at least another dozen.

"Even if you actually believed that, you know that Claude is better for you. He would do anything for you. There wasn't a day that went by where he didn't think about you. He regretted not being able to find you that day—he even risked his life to search for you before the bombing. Then afterward, he searched and searched for you. He didn't want to give up hope, but I forced him to come into the mountains with the rest of us. I had even given up hope. Every time a party went down to gather supplies for the winter, he would tell them to keep an eye out for you. Why can't you see he is a better match for you?"

Ellie glanced at me, then turned back to her brother. "I never said he wasn't. I just said that I don't love him the way I love Cor."

"Then you truly are a fool."

"I'm trying," she whispered. "I want to love him more than I love Cor. I really do. It's just going to take time."

"Then stop being an idiot and saying stuff like that. He cares for you, but he worries that you will leave him. Just…" He pinched the bridge of his nose. "I love you, sister, I really do. But just don't toy with his heart, okay? He deserves better than that.”

“I know he does.”

There was a knock at the door. Edmund opened it. It was Claude.

“The elders want to see us now. All four of us.”

Edmund nodded and led us back to the room we first went to when we arrived at this fortress. People were beginning to wake up for the day and watched us as we made our way to the council room. I worried what they would say or do to us and what they wanted to do with Gabe. It wasn’t Gabe’s fault—any of us would have done the same in his position. He’d watched that Kausian kill his mother.

We came upon the council room and found all the elders waiting for us. They looked tired and angry. Whether the anger was because they were awakened in the middle of the night or because they were dealing with us again. Probably a bit of both.

“Please take a seat,” Mae said.

All four of us did as was asked of us. I glanced at Ellie he seemed to be the most worried. She had kept secrets, horrible secrets, and I doubted they were going to take any of that lightly.

Marvin said, "We have much to discuss here today and much to decide. But first we would like to hear from you all as to what has happened."

We all glanced at one another as if debating who should go first.

"Elvira, how about you start from the beginning since you seem to know more than anyone what happened."

Ellie took a deep breath, then let it out slowly. "Fine, sure. I guess we have to start somewhere. Some three years ago, Cor was tricked into giving the codes to someone name Byron. He gave those codes to the Silurians, who then destroyed our home. Cor ran off and tried to get close to Krax so he could kill him. Meanwhile, Zach and I became bounty hunters trying to find Cor. Cor also teamed up with Gabe. Gabe is the son of the Byron's brother and the Sirian queen, making him a prince. We finally found Cor, and while we were figuring out what happened, Byron set us up to destroy the Silurians.

"We found out Byron was the one behind it all and is trying to destroy all the races so that humans can rule the planet. He wants us all to destroy each other so humans won't die in the crossfire. He set up his son for the murder of the Sirian queen using a Kausian transformed as him—the Kausian in the infirmary. We escaped but got arrested once we set foot on land. We all escaped except Cor, and Cor got taken by Byron to his manor—the same manor that Gabe's father lived in. Gabe decided he would contact his father to stop Byron. We snuck into the manor only to find that Gabe's father was the mastermind behind it all, and he killed Byron and tried to kill us. We managed to escape and traveled to these forests only to find you all. Does that sum it up?"

Ellie did a good job simplifying it all—and glossing over the monstrosities that Cor had committed. I debated if I should say anything, but I had a feeling that would make Gabe appear worse since he had traveled with Cor. It would appear that perhaps he was part of Cor hunting down Kausians for Krax, which I had a hard time believing. He wasn't like that.

The elders all glanced at one another, then turned back to Ellie. "Then explain the past day what happened."

"We were on watch when we saw the Kausian

come in—the one who killed the Sirian queen—and Cor got scared, so he made his escape, leaving all of us behind."

"But you knew he was leaving."

Ellie's lip twitched. "Yes."

"And you didn't say anything? Knowing that we don't let people leave here due to security."

"He isn't going to tell anyone where we are."

"Do you know that for a fact?" Mae asked. "He has betrayed our people before; why do you think he won't do it again to save his own skin?"

Ellie was silent.

"Then your friend tried to murder the Kausian," Melvin added.

I answered quickly, "Because he killed his mother. You can't blame him for that."

"We don't know for a fact he wasn't working for his father or for his uncle. We also don't know how much he was involved with Cor when he was hunting his own people, now do we? For all you know, this could be a setup," Melvin responded.

I shook my head. "He isn't like that. He was just taking revenge for his mother."

"And how far will his revenge go, hmm? Does he blame all Kausians for her death? The fact we can shape-shift? That is how it all started—too many people blamed us for things that happened due to our shape-shifting abilities."

We were all silent.

"You four are dismissed. We will discuss what you have revealed further and come for you. In the meantime, get some food and wait in your quarters."

We all nodded, and Edmund led us away.

CHAPTER III

Cor

It was cold. I was tired. But I kept running.

I knew I was going down the mountain—I could feel the incline under my feet—but it felt as if there was no end in sight. All I could make out were trees and bushes, and that was when I got close to them. It was dark, I felt as if I would freeze to death, and I didn't know if I was going to survive this. Should I have stayed? If I had explained myself, would they have forgiven me? Would my fate be better there than out here?

No. No one would have taken my side in any of this. I had made a lot of bad decision in the past three years, and I doubted anyone would have agreed with any of them, except perhaps Ellie. For some reason she always saw the good in me even though I didn't deserve it. She was always like that. I would lose count how many times she had saved my ass. She was good at getting out of tough situations, where as I usually got the shit beaten out of me. She was probably one of the reasons I made it to 18.

I had tried to do her right by wanting to go to a human university. Byron had promised me a spot in one of the most prestigious universities. I should have known it was too good to be true. I should have known better than to trust an outsider. The one time I thought of someone other than myself and it blew up in my face.

But even after that, I made a lot of bad decisions. I worked for Krax, killing my own kind. There was no coming back from that. I claimed I had done it because I was trying to seek revenge, but I could have simply disappeared or helped the Kausians recover. No one knew it was me that had given the codes except Ellie. I could have found our people and helped rebuild a nation. I could have found Ellie and explained everything to her. Instead, I was selfish and found myself in this mess. Not only did I not have my revenge, but Krax had been killed by Byron, and Byron had been killed by his brother. I was left nothing and only brought misery to the people around me.

And none of them deserved to have to deal with me.

Gabe deserved better than me. I'd dragged him all across Mu, and he ended up losing his mother and finding out his father was a monster. If I hadn't been with him, well, he probably would have been killed already by Byron, so perhaps he wasn't a good example. He would have been pulled into the middle of this mess with or without me. But I still felt as if I had caused him more pain than needed—especially since I just had left him behind with a bunch of strangers. Sure he had Ellie and Zach, but he only met them a few days ago.

Then there was Zach. Zach would have been happier as he wouldn't have to deal with my shit, and that included before the attack on Kaus. He was sort of just included in everything we did. He never wanted to do the things we did, but he always tagged along since he didn't want to be left out. Perhaps, as teenagers, we took that for granted. And Ellie…

Ellie deserved someone like Claude.

Claude was there for her. He didn't run when things got rough. He didn't bring on the destruction of Kaus. He didn't become a bounty hunter and kill his own kind. No, he wanted to live a peaceful life in Kaus and treat Ellie well. He always loved her, but I had been in the way of that. I tried to keep her away from him when I could, in fear that he would make a move on her and she would realize he was a decent man compared to me. But if she had picked him, then she could have lived a happy life. I wouldn't have gone to Byron to get tutoring, and Kaus wouldn't have been destroyed.

I ruined everything just by existing.

Well, now Ellie and Claude could be together and not deal with me. Odds were I was going to die out here, or at least, odds were I would never be allowed back to anything Kaus related and she could live happily ever after. They all could. Well, at least as happily ever after as they could in hiding. It was sure a lot better up there than it was on the rest of Mu.

Because the rest of Mu was going to be at war.

I wondered how long the war would last and whether Jonathan would get his wish, and the humans would take over the entire world. While I knew a lot of humans who weren't as sadistic or cruel as Jonathan and Byron, I really hoped that wouldn't happen. There were plenty of Lyrans and Sirians that were kind as well. There weren't many Silurians who were kind, so I didn't really care what happened to them. They were the ones who'd led the attack on Kaus after all.

As I ran, I felt my foot catch on something, and I tumbled down. I hit the snow with a soft thud. The coldness touched my face as it met with the cold snow. Tears mixed with the melted snow.

I had messed up. I had lost everything. Just when I thought, perhaps, I had paid my karma, it came back to bite me in the ass yet again. I thought maybe I could finally live my life, only to find myself cold and alone.

Slamming my fist on the ground, I screamed. The scream echoed through the area, only to fade away as no sound followed.

"This isn't fair. None of this is fair."

I sat there for a long moment before gathering myself again. I stood up and headed back down the mountain.

Time passed and I came across some familiar areas. Even in the dark with my flashlight, I was able to recognize some of the trees and lake. I was close to where we had made camp earlier.

Which meant I had somewhere to rest for the night.

I retraced my steps to where I remembered the camp was to find that it was still standing, albeit cold. Luckily no big storm had hit yet as it was still the end of the summer and the crisp, autumn air was just beginning to settle in. I couldn't imagine what these mountains were like in the winter, and I was sort of glad I was running away now rather than deal with any of that. I hated the cold and was very much a summer boy. Granted, I did like cuddling with Ellie on cold nights in the Kausian desert, but although that was chilly, we never had to deal with snow.

There was some wood for the fire in the middle of the makeshift cabin we had. I checked the cabin and found there were still a couple of fire starters left over from the cabin we had found earlier. I lit the fire in the middle of the floor and watched as the smoke traveled up the chimney we'd created.

Turning off the flashlight, I let the fire light up the room. Everything that we didn't care about was where we'd left it. I sat down on the bed and leaned forward on my knees, staring at the orange and red glow.

What would have happened if we hadn't run into Edmund and Claude that day? What would have happened if we had stayed here? Would we have survived? Would we have been happy? It could have just been the four of us, and we could have been happy, right? Or would we have died a cold and cruel death? I knew it was probably the latter, but I wanted to believe that wasn't so. I wanted to believe perhaps in another life we could have been happy.

But the cards were never in our favor.

If I hadn't given the codes to Byron, he would have killed me or he would have kidnapped Ellie and forced me to give him the codes. I knew he would go to such lengths. All this would still have happened—there was nothing any of us could have done to prevent it. Byron and his brother had been weaving this tapestry for a long while, and we were mere tools of his creation. And yet it seemed as if I kept making the wrong decision over and over again.

How was I going to make any of this right?

CHAPTER IV

Gabe

I really messed up this time, and I didn't know how I was going to get out of it.

Although the cell was rudimentary—nothing like the one we been thrown in when were arrested in the Human Zone—it wasn't as if I had anywhere to go, not to mention the terrain I would escape to worried me. There was no way I would be able to survive out there. I had no idea how to harvest foods or hunt, especially in snow so thick. Those weren't exactly things princes were taught—especially a Sirian one.

So I waited for what was next. I had a feeling they were going to sentence me to death, and I couldn't really blame them. I had betrayed their trust by trying to kill one of their own instead of telling the elders what had happened. Maybe I could have gotten some sympathy that way, although I doubted they would have done anything to the Kausians. He was under Byron's control at the time, but I still couldn't help myself. I wanted him to pay for what he'd done.

And now I was alone in this place, and I had dragged Ellie and Zach down with me. The Kausians were going to blame them for what happened since they trusted me. It was my fault they were being questioned now.

Then there was Cor. He had left me behind—he had left us all behind. He should have told me. He should have come for me, and we could have left together. He should have known that I would have wanted revenge or that he could have identified me and taken all of us down with him. Instead, he'd just run off on his own. Again.

I was such a fool, thinking he would stay by my

side.

Ellie and Zach had warned me, and I had noticed all the signs. He always seemed like he was ready to go. He was using me for my money and connections. I had hoped for more, but, alas, some people never change.

After a while of sulking, one of the elders came to my cell along with some young, stronger men. The elder was Mae. Her gray hair was disheveled and she appeared as tired as I was. I caused these people a lot of problems in the past day, and I felt horrible about it.

"We are bringing you before the council. Please do not resist."

I nodded. "Don't worry, I don't plan on trying to escape."

Mae gestured to the men who were with her and they opened the cell. Each one of them grabbed a different arm and they led me toward the council room which, of course was on the other side of the settlement.

I wasn't sure how many of these people knew of what happened, but enough seemed to have an inkling that I had betrayed them. They glared at me, and if it weren't for Mae being present, I had a feeling they would yell at me and come at me with pitchforks.

This place was starting to feel like home.

We entered the council chambers, and Mae gestured to a seat as she took a seat next to the rest of the council. "Please take a seat."

I did as she asked, my wrists still bound before me.

"We would like to take your account of what happened. Please start from the beginning."

"Beginning of what? Me attacking the Kausian, beginning my adventure with Cor, or when I was born?" I asked.

She waved her hand. "Start wherever it feels appropriate."

I took a deep breath and let it out slowly. "The very beginning it is then. All of this will make more sense that way, but I will summarize to keep it short. I grew up with my people hating me. They didn't like that I was half human. My uncle tormented me and told me I should never have been born. He turned my people against me and more than once tried to have me killed. I never really knew my father. A little over two years ago I ran away from home. I didn't know what I would do, but I knew I needed to get away before Byron got his wish. I stumbled upon Cor one day—he was in a bit of trouble as he always is—and the two of us decided to team up and watch each other's backs, albeit it we didn't know we were doing that for each other at the time."

"In what way did you team up?" Mae asked.

I shrugged. "He was already sleeping around for money. I just became his partner and found him clientele. I screened them to make sure no trouble would arise. He often got into some trouble with the people he slept with. Or, better yet, he got in trouble with their partners."

"Was this on top of the bounty hunter work he was doing for the Silurian Krax?" Mae asked.

I shook my head. "I didn't know about any of that until today, or last night I should say."

"You didn't notice he was bounty hunting on the side?"

"No. He would leave for some periods of time, but I didn't know that was what he was doing. We both had secrets, as he didn't know I was a Sirian prince. We didn't pry into each other's personal life too much."

"What happened after that?"

"Well." I sighed. "I guess after that Ellie and Zach were hired by Byron to kill me or at least bring me to him, which would also end with my death. They realized I knew where Cor was, so they spared my life and pissed off my uncle. Then we all went to Zynon because that was where Cor was only to find that Byron was setting up the Silurians so that all the countries would begin a war on them. Then we escaped and went to the Sirian Zone. There, we tried to convince my mother that Byron was doing all of this, which she believed us and was going to reveal to everyone what had happened on Zynon when Byron used the Kausian you have in the infirmary to kill my mother. The Kausian transformed into me and murdered my mother to make everyone think I did it. Do you understand how cruel that was?"

No one answered, so I carried on with my story.

"The we escaped to the Human Zone where we were captured. We were able to escape. That is... well, except for Cor. Byron came for Cor and took him to my father's mansion. So, I decided to talk to my father to see if he would stop all this nonsense. Little did I know my father was really the one behind it all and was using Byron to do all the dirty work. He tried to murder me, but we were able to escape to the mountains. That was when we ran into Claude and Edmund. And that brings us to the present day."

The council each glanced at one another, as if either debating on believing my story, or confirming the story Ellie and Zach told them, if they had already told them story. I was guessing they met with them before me.

"Did you know Cor was going to abandon this place?" Mae asked.

I shook my head. "No. If I did, I would have joined him."

"So, you are saying you would run away, ignore the hospitality we gave you, and put all our lives in jeopardy?"

"No, not like that. Because one of your people used my likeness to kill my own mother. What would you have done if you ran into that person? You can't tell me you wouldn't have tried to kill them."

"As you said yourself, they were forced to by Byron."

"Yeah, but I am sure you all want Cor dead as well. Do you blame him, or do you blame Byron?"

I asked.

They all glanced at one another. Mae answered, "It is a little more complicated than that. If Cor came to us after it all happened, maybe we could have done something. Instead, he tried to take matters into his own hands and killed his own people in the process. These two matters are not the same."

I frowned. I didn't like where this was going.

"We are a close-knit community due to the other nations committing genocide against our people. We welcomed you into this community with the assumption you would follow our rules and not cause any problems. Had you come to us letting us know the situation, we could have dealt with this matter in a more diplomatic way. However, you decided to betray us and kill one of our own instead of telling us the truth. We must take care of our people and keep them safe from outsiders. We have decided you must be terminated. We will give you some time to say your goodbyes to Ellie and Zach, but you will be sentenced to death."

I stared at her, not believing what I was hearing. This couldn't be possible.

CHAPTER V

Ellie

Edmund decided to take Zach back to our cabin, and Claude took me back to their cabin. Zach was still angry at me, which I understood. We had been friends for years and I had kept Cor's secret from him. Edmund was also still pretty upset with me, but that was typically for him. He hated Cor, and this wasn't our first fight about him. But I hadn't run away with him and stayed here to build a life with Claude, so that should have meant something.

I also wanted to take this time to talk to Claude. He was probably also upset with me and that I hadn't told anyone about Cor, but could anyone really blame me? He would have been killed on the spot had any of these people known. Besides, I could tell it was eating him up inside. He felt guilt beyond what anyone of us could imagine.

Not only that, but I honestly didn't want to believe he was a bounty hunter. I didn't want to believe he had killed others. I wanted to believe that he was innocent, and it had been all of Byron and Jonathan's fault. But Cor was also to blame— he didn't have to do missions for Krax. He could have talked to us. We would have figured something out.

We made it back to the set of cabins, but not with some questioning gazes following us. It was a small settlement, and I was sure the truth was already making its way through the rumor mills. How many lies people added I wasn't sure, but I was sure it was plenty. It wasn't as if we were innocent, but things in Kaus were often spun to make the three of us look even worse, and I doubted those things had changed.

Claude and I were silent as we entered the cabin.

I sat down on the bed, and he sat on the bed across from me. I was tired, as were all of us. There was so much I wanted to tell him—to make him understand—but no words to help the situation came to my mind.

"Was all that stuff you said true?" Claude asked. "Have you really been dealing with people trying to kill you for the past couple of weeks?"

I let out a breath. "And then some. But we found Cor two weeks before we arrived here. The attack on Zynon, the attack on the Sirians, and the whole thing with Gabe's father was all within a two-week period, yes."

"And before that?" Claude asked. "What really went on?"

I shrugged. "Zach and I did what we had to. We tried to make a home for ourselves, but bandits kept attacking us. So, we became bounty hunters. We turned people in for the crimes they committed or at least they said they committed. We always had to run from city to city since people didn't like Kausians being bounty hunters. We got into trouble a lot."

He grabbed my hand and caressed it with his thumb. "That must have been hard, especially when you thought you were all alone."

"We ran into some Kausians but none that wanted anything to do with us. We really did feel alone, but Zach and I were used to being outsiders. Besides you and my brother, we didn't exactly get along with many others. We just… struggled when it came to having to deal with other nations, which was all the time."

"I know I've said this before, but I'm sorry you were alone all this time. Had I known…"

I shook my head. "It's not your fault. My brother told me you searched for me as long as you could, and you had people keep an eye out when they went into town."

"No, I could have done more. I could have kept searching."

"No, you didn't know I was alive. It could have all been for nothing. So many people died—I mean, I assumed you and Edmund were dead."

"But not Cor?" he asked. "You didn't assume he was dead?"

I hesitated. "I… I knew Cor was alive. He… he was the reason Zach and I survived. He warned us, in a way, so I knew he'd gotten out alive. Both Zach and I decided to hunt him down and find out what really happened. I assumed since he knew the attack was coming that he had something to do with it. Had I known all of it…"

"And after you found out everything, you still love him?"

I looked away. "I… I don't know. We were together for so long. Maybe my brother was right—maybe he had always been right. Cor gets into trouble, and I end up having to save his ass. And even then, if it gets too rough…"

"He runs off."

I slowly nodded. "So I guess I need to just stop being delusional and accept that the two of us aren't on the same page. I will stand and fight and he will always cower with his tail between his legs, not caring who he leaves behind."

He was silent, as if processing it all.

"And on top of it all, he left Gabe behind, and now he is up for attempted murder," I added. "I know that he would never be there for me in the end. But that is hard to digest, even after all this time."

"So then what are you going to do now?" Claude asked.

I shrugged. "I… I guess we wait to see what the

elders decide."

Claude frowned. "I don't think it is going to be good. Gabe showed an act of hostility toward a Kausian, and he is not a Kausian himself. We don't often get into fights, so I doubt anyone is going to have any sympathy for him even if the Kausian did kill his mother. Not to mention not many were happy he was here in the first place."

I let my breath out slowly. "And what about Zach and me?"

"I… I don't know. You not only brought the Sirian here, but you also knew what Cor had done and didn't say anything. It doesn't look good."

I stared down at the wood planks that made up the floor. "Do you think they will sentence all of us to death?"

He shook his head. "I won't let that happen."

"You know it's likely though."

"I know that Edmund and I are highly thought of by the council, and they will listen to us."

"Then we will just be prisoners. The two of us will always be watched and everyone will be suspicious. We won't be accepted."

Claude ran his hands through his dark hair. "Then what would you have me do, Ellie? I don't want to see you leave—not again. Not after thinking you were dead for so long."

I grabbed his hand. "Then come with me. You and Edmund and Zach—we could all just leave. We could break Gabe out and just make a run for it. There are plenty of places we can make a life at. Shit, with all of us, perhaps we could even stop Jonathan."

"Are you crazy? We can't leave this place. And the five of us wouldn't be able to stop Jonathan, not that any of the other zones deserve us helping them. They stood by and watched as the Silurians level our city to the ground."

"Don't you want a home to go back to? Or do you want to live in this cave the rest of your life?"

"We have been living here for three years. It's not as bad as you think. We were able to make a home here."

"It will never be a home to us—not when we will always be questioned as to our loyalty. You see that right? Even when I told them what happened, they looked at us like outsiders. Living here is not going to be an option. Tensions will rise—they always do. I've seen it before."

"And you think anywhere else will accept us?

Believe me when I say it takes a village, Ellie. You have been on the run all this time. You know they won't accept us anywhere. I think you are just scared of finally staying still, or perhaps you just want to leave here so you can find Cor."

I shook my head. "No. That's not it. I want to belong. I really do. I thought we had something. Claude… I chose to stay here. I could have made a run for it with Cor. But I… I wanted a real life." I squeezed his hand. "I want something that would be stable. I want my home again."

He smiled a little but then let out a defeated laugh. "But now you are saying you can't have that."

"No, I can't. Because they no longer trust us. I had hoped he wouldn't have said those things—I had hoped he would have never found out Cor was here."

"So then no one would find out the secrets you were hiding? Is that it?"

"In essence, yes. I mean, can you blame me? So much has happened. Horrible decisions were made, people died… and no, I can't forgive Cor for everything he has done, just like I can't be forgiven for everything I have done."

"You haven't—"

"Save it. That is a lie. I know I have turned in people who were probably innocent. I know that I have worked for criminals. I have led to people's deaths the same as Cor did in order to survive. It is no different."

Claude was silent for a long moment. I let out a sigh.

"It doesn't matter. They are going to either have us killed or drop us off somewhere in the middle of the mountain to die. Either way, it doesn't look good."

"Just… Just promise me you will come to me before you do anything stupid, okay? We will figure this out together. I won't let anything happen to you—you understand?"

I nodded. "Thank you, Claude. I mean it. I am glad I finally have someone I can rely on and not worry will leave me. Other than Zach, of course."

"You can always rely on me, Ellie. I promise you that. Now get some sleep if you can. Today is going to be a long day."

CHAPTER VI

Zach

I could tell this was all going to end horribly.

It was clear the council of elders wasn't going to let Gabe go, and it was clear they didn't trust Ellie nor me—and with good reason. We had been harboring a fugitive—one that had destroyed our own people. But it wasn't as if we could exactly tell them what happened. How would one betray their friend like that? While he and I go into our arguments, I couldn't exactly hand him over to his death. Not after everything we had faced in the past two weeks, let alone our entire lives. We had always watched each other's backs, even if it meant keeping a secret here and there.

Edmund sat on Ellie's bed—frustrated as I was at everything that had transpired. He and I had a lot in common—mainly having to deal with Ellie's and Cor's shenanigans. We bonded over the fact he was Ellie's brother, and I felt like a brother to her when we were younger. He also felt like a brother to me —I brother I wish I had at home. He was protective and had always been there for me when my mother when on one of her drunken rampages and I needed a place to stay for the night. He always made me feel welcomed, and for that I was thankful.

"I don't know how you stuck around with her all this time—she can be quite impossible. I'm stuck with her because of blood, but you chose to. I don't know how you do it," Edmund commented.

I shrugged. "While she can be impossible, she has a heart of gold and won't back down from a fight. She's brave and loyal and will never leave her friends behind. Unlike that someone she likes to keep around."

"I just don't get it. Why can't she see that he's

holding her back? That he would never do the same things for her as she would do, or has done, for him?"

"I don't get it either. They have some weird bond… He keeps leaving her, and yet she still loves him. While I still care for him as a friend, I don't feel like ever chasing him again. He can just go live his own life or self-destruct for all I care."

"If I am honest, I think Claude deserves better. He deserves someone who won't be always thinking about someone else and what-if scenarios," Edmund said.

"Then they are a lot alike—they both are striving after people who they will never fully have."

Edmund let out a laugh. "I guess then, in that way, they are perfect for one another."

We sat there in silence once again. I debated if I should try to sleep, but I knew with everything going on, I wouldn't be able to quiet my mind. I was truly tired, though.

"Do you think they will let him go?" I asked. "Gabe, I mean."

Edmund shook his head. "If I am being honest, I doubt it. He is an outsider, and he tried to murder someone in the community. While I definitely understand why he wanted to kill that man, the council is going to question whether he would do it again or if you all are carrying any other secrets."

I shook my head. "Ellie and I won't let him die."

"Then you are going to have to take extreme measures to stop them. Honestly, if you did anything and got caught, you will be sentenced to death as well."

"You think we won't be already?" I asked. "You think they aren't trying to determine what to do with us? They aren't going to let us wander around on our own. Odds are they are going to punish us the same or are going to be watching our every move like we are prisoners."

"Isn't being a prisoner better than being dead?"

I shook my head. "No. Not when you can be free. While Ellie and I were always on the run, it was probably the best time we had because we didn't have to follow anyone's rule or have to worry about the greater good of our kind. We did what we needed to do and could go wherever we wanted. We got to be ourselves and didn't have to worry about the repercussion on Kaus."

"Didn't you miss having a community?"

I shrugged. "Yes, and the past few days have

been great but… it's just not the same. Seeing the world and moving around… it gave us a sense of freedom. I miss having a family, but I also miss looking out at the stars on a warm summer's night. I don't miss being here where people are judging me because I'm only half Kausian."

Edmund frowned. "Are people still giving you a hard time?"

"I don't know. I don't think so, but the fear is still there—as if they are just waiting for an excuse to kick me out. No one has approached me like they used to, but I also don't feel as welcomed as the others. Perhaps I am just imagining it."

"No, if you feel that way, it is completely valid. They were harsh to you back then, especially as a child. You didn't deserve it, and I wouldn't put it past any of them to pull the same stunts they did back then. While I like to think our people are better because of what happened, I don't have any proof to back that up. I am sorry for what they did to you."

I smiled a little. "Thank you. I appreciate it. Truly."

There was a knocking at the door, and Edmund stood up to open it. It was Claude. He was frowning.

"What is it?" Edmund asked.

"The council has decided Gabe's fate."

"What is it?" I asked. "What did they decide?"

Claude eyed me, as if trying to find the right words. "They decided he should be executed. They have found him to be a threat and have decided he can't be let go in fear he will tell his father where we are."

I shook my head. "No, they can't. He didn't do anything wrong! It's not his fault that his father is evil. He is the purest person out there!"

"I'm sorry, it's not up to me. It's the council's decision," Claude added. "I don't want him dead either, but we can't exactly go against the council."

I stood up and began pacing around. "How long do we have?"

"Until tomorrow morning. But he is under heavy security. You won't be able to break him out of there even if you tried."

I tried to think of a plan but couldn't come up with any ideas. "And what about Ellie and me?"

"You two will have to stay here. You will always have a guard of some sort."

"Great. We will have people loathe us because

we have to always be watched."

He shrugged. "I don't think they will be that strict with you two. Or, at least, not after a while."

"So we will be prisoners in our own home. Great."

"It's better than the alternative," Claude said.

"The alternative that our friend is facing now?"

He didn't say anything.

"Can I speak to Ellie?" I asked.

Claude shook his head. "No. We have been ordered to keep you two apart until after tomorrow."

Because they knew we would try to save him and escape. They thought of everything. I glanced at Edmund. "Are you just going to let them kill our friend and treat us like prisoners too?"

Edmund looked away. "Our hands are tied, Zach. I can't do anything. This is honestly the best-case scenario—it could have been a lot worse."

No, the best-case scenario would have been if the elders simply kicked us all out, but I understood their reason. We could have been captured and tortured, and we would have given away this location. Or they feared we would simply give it to anyone because we had been kicked out.

But they were fools to think they could stop us from trying to save Gabe.

Ellie was alone right now, or at least I believed she was. I listened closely since the door was open to the outside and the house she was in wasn't that far. That's when I heard it—tapping.

Ellie did have a plan, and I knew exactly what she wanted me to do.

CHAPTER VII

Cor

I woke up as the fire in the hut began smoldering. I didn't think I was going to actually fall asleep, but after a few long blinks, I opened my eyes to daylight.

I was still in the mountains, but at least I made it through the night—that was the hard part. And since I'd found our hut, I knew exactly where I was. I could get down the mountain if I was quick, which I needed to be, as I didn't want to spend another moment in this cold terrain.

Taking a deep breath, I let it out slowly. I wished I was still asleep as I was having a dream about Ellie. We were in Kaus, living the life we would never get to live. I wished more than anything I could go back in time and simply undo what I had done. We could have just lived a simple life in Kaus. I could have taken over for my parents and she could have found work in town or with her brother on the farm. But I always wanted more and look where that led.

There was no use in moping around like this. I stood up and gathered any supplies we might have left that I could use on my journey down the mountain. It wasn't much, but any little help could make all the difference. And if I did make it to town, then I could sell whatever I had left—granted if my face wasn't plastered on every wall, which was always possible, even before crossing Jonathan like we had.

I still couldn't believe that Jonathan was the one pulling the strings this whole time. He let his brother do all the dirty work just so he could come in at the end and take over whatever he had planned. It was devious to say the least.

Which meant this whole time, I had been chasing the wrong person.

I had originally thought it was Krax who was pulling the strings, as that was what Byron had led me to believe when he was mentoring. He always acted like Krax was up to something devious, and it had been Krax who had kidnapped me and threatened Ellie for the codes. Then, after getting close to Krax, I discover it was Byron who was controlling him and watch as Byron murdered the person I had spent the past three years trying to destroy. Then, after making it my mission to take out Byron, his brother kills him. It wasn't fair—I had wasted the past three years of my life doing things I would always regret with nothing to show for it.

So I had to kill Jonathan if it was the last thing I did.

The problem was, if I killed him, Jonathan had already said he would just be a martyr, and a martyr's ideals were stronger than someone's who was alive. This let me not knowing what to do next.

I had time to think about it, however, as I still had another day of travel to get off this mountain, if not longer. It all depended on if I remembered the best way out or not. While I knew I needed to go down, that didn't necessarily mean I remembered the best way down. I could end up on a cliffside or something and have to go all the way around, as there was no way I was going to scale down a cliff in these icy conditions.

Eating part of the last protein pack I could find, I started my journey down the mountainside. Luckily there weren't many creatures wandering these woods—mainly because they were so treacherous no animals wanted to be here. Either way, I had a loaded gun, so if it came to it, I could defend myself against a bear or any other beast that was roaming the area. I didn't want to hurt them, however, as this was their territory, not mine. But I would defend myself if need be.

It was quiet. I listened for any sound other than the snow crunching under my boot, but there was nothing. I didn't even hear birds or squirrels rustling in the bushes. It was eerie and yet serene. I could understand why my people would make a home up here—it was quiet, and there was no fear that some other nation was going to attack.

We had lived in horrible conditions in the desert. In the winter, it was freezing at night, and in the summer, there was escape from the heat of the two suns. It was no wonder that the Silurians just decided to destroy the area instead of taking it for themselves, although they had the technology to have air conditioning and heating in all of their buildings.

All of us Kausians wanted to live somewhere better—but there was just no other hospitable land. Which was why they could make a life in these mountains—we were used to having to fight all sorts of weather, albeit we weren't used to the snow, but the clearly had made it work.

I wondered if Byron, or Jonathan, ever sent people to look for Kausians out here or if he figured it would be a lost cause. He had to focus on taking out the other nations—it wasn't as if out here the Kausians could put together an army or get any help, and it wasn't as if anyone would help out our kind. No, we were exactly where they wanted us, if they even thought we were alive.

So, question was, would they come looking and attack the settlement after the war that was coming?

I hoped it wouldn't come to that—I hoped that someone would stop Jonathan before any more war transpired. Problem was, it was clear that no one was going to stop him. The Silurians were losing their war. The Sirians were going to ignore what was happening on land and keep to themselves. The only hope was the Lyrans, and I had no idea what their view was in all this, other than they probably had sent forces against the Silurians as no other nation liked or trusted them. The Lyrans were a proud race, but they often kept to themselves. They didn't care for Sirians, and no one really liked the Silurians—so what were they going to do? And how was Jonathan going to start a war with them?

I still didn't know what I was going to do once I got off this mountain. It wasn't as if I had anywhere to go. I didn't have anyone I could trust with me. I was completely alone. Just like I had been three years ago.

I should have convinced Ellie to come with me or went and got Gabe. But they deserved better. Ellie had Claude now, and those two deserved each other. And I couldn't keep making Gabe run every time a ghost of my past came to haunt me. They probably all hated me now, and the truth would come out that I had been a bounty hunter against our own kind.

I was despicable.

I could forgive myself for trusting Byron, but the things I did after were what really caused me to stay awake at night. And it all had been for nothing. Krax hadn't been the one who was behind it all. I had led to the deaths of dozens of Kausians just because I had been a selfish fool.

Part of me wanted to stop where I was and let the snow take me, but I knew that would be a mistake. I had to right my wrongs if it was the last thing I would do.

The day went on, and nothing attacked me, animal or Kausian, as I descended down the mountain. Apparently, I had a better sense of direction than I thought and had picked the correct way down the mountain. Although my legs ached and my fingers began to feel numb, I kept on walking, praying to the goddess that I had been going the correct way. A few hours passed and I noticed that the the snow was getting shallower and shallower as I went. I was going the right way—I was almost in the clear.

I was beginning to have hope again.

CHAPTER VIII

Gabe

I was going to die. This was it.

There were two people standing outside the cell, making sure I wouldn't try anything—as if I could do anything. I didn't know how to get out of this cell, and I wasn't exactly that great at hand-to-hand combat. That was Cor's forte, while I was good at… well, something. I guess I was good at usually staying out of trouble, although that wasn't true these past two weeks. It felt as if all my running had caught up to me, and everything was spiraling out of control.

It didn't matter anymore—tomorrow I would be put to death, however that would be, and that would be the end of it. At least then I would see my mother in the afterlife, and we could be together again. I wouldn't have to deal with my people hating me or my father trying to kill me any longer. It would just be me and my mother in the afterlife.

I rubbed my face. Why was I so weak? Why couldn't I keep myself safe? I always had to rely on others to save me, and I really doubted anyone was going to save me now. Cor was gone—he left me behind to escape, well, all of this. Then Ellie and Zach couldn't exactly save me—not without compromising themselves. These were their people —they weren't going to run away from this place. They weren't going to risk everything just to save me. And I couldn't blame them. They had been searching for somewhere to belong and this was it.

This was all my fault. Why had I been so stupid? Why did I think it would be an okay thing to kill someone? It wasn't his fault he was used by Byron —we all had been used by Byron. I shouldn't have tried to kill him—it was wrong.

But I couldn't get the image out of my head of him transforming himself into me and then assassinating my mother.

The worst part of all this was that I was alone. I had no one to talk to—no one to tell my story. Zach had been there with me when my mother was killed. He understood. All those people should have understood, but instead, they decided to eliminate what they considered a threat.

Cor should have taken me with him—he knew what that Kausian did. Why did he think I would be fine living in the same community as him? He should have known better. We could have been long gone, Ellie and Zach could have stayed here and found a place where they belonged, and none of this would have happened.

I needed to stop thinking of what-ifs and focus on the now. How was I going to get out of here? How was I going to save myself from this mess? Even if I did escape, how was I going to make it all the way down the mountain? I didn't know the first thing about surviving in the snow, not to mention I was passed out for most of the time. I grew up in the water—I barely knew how to survive on the surface, let alone the mountains. Now if this were all underwater, that would be a different story.

The day went by, and I was brought meals. They were the standard meals handed out during the potlucks, which I was thankful for—they couldn't have easily just served my slop or nothing at all. The guards didn't say much, but nor would they look me in the eye. I wondered what all the citizens thought about the elders' decision and whether they agreed or understood why I did what I did. I was too afraid to ask.

It was the middle of the day when I heard someone outside my cell. I stood up to find the last face I thought I would ever see. Well, second-to-last face.

"It's you," I whispered to the Kausian who had killed my mother.

"Yeah. It's me."

We both stood there for a moment, staring at one another. I had no idea why he was here, and I wasn't sure how I felt about it. My blood felt as if it were beginning to boil, and I could hardly breath. At the same time, my heart felt as if it were skipping a beat—hopefully of he might say.

What could he possibly say to make this better? Who was I kidding?

"I know there is nothing I can say to make things right," he commented at last. "And I wanted to let you know I am doing everything I can to stop this."

I wasn't sure what I expected him to say, but it wasn't that. "I… um… Thanks, I guess?"

"You don't deserve to die for trying to kill me. I get it. I would do the same if I were in your shoes. But the council… they aren't as open-minded. They fear… well, they fear for the people. There aren't many of us left, and the fact you were traveling with Cornelius… That's not helping."

I frowned. I still couldn't believe what they said was true. Cor was hunting Kausians on the side. How did I not have noticed? We both had our secrets, but it would explain why he would disappears days at a time.

"Do you know what will happen to my friends? Ellie and Zach?"

He shrugged. "They will stay in this compound until the council decides they aren't a threat, however long that will take. They are being watched carefully and probably will be until the day they die."

They weren't going to like that, but at least they weren't going to be killed for something I did.

"Ah. That's good, I guess."

The man looked down and shook his head. "I am sorry. For everything. Byron had me locked up for weeks… torturing me. I am lucky to be alive… but… that is still no excuse. I should have run for it or stopped it. I'm sorry."

I didn't want to forgive him, but I knew I was placing all my hatred for my uncle and father on someone who was closer to me—someone who was a lot more easily obtainable.

"I forgive you. I'm sorry I tried to kill you. I know it was Byron's fault. We are all just puppets. Well, Jonathan's puppets now."

He furrowed his brow. "What do you mean?"

"Jonathan. He killed Byron. He was really the one pulling the strings. He made it appear like Byron was a martyr and was going on to fulfill his brother's wishes. Everything was a setup. My birth was even a setup to take down the Sirians. He used me. He used my mother. He used all of us. I'm not sure how we will stop him—well, I guess I won't have to worry about that."

I felt tears swell up in my eyes. We were all just pawns. They didn't see any of us as actual human beings. We were disposable.

"That is… unnerving to say the least. Byron mentioned you were his nephew, but I had no idea that you were also part of their plan. I can't even imagine… I'm sorry."

"Thank you. And again, I shouldn't have done what I did. I just saw red and suddenly was over your bed…"

"Again, I understand. I would have done the same if I were you." He stepped back. "I will do what I can to convince the council they are wrong. I promise."

With that, he left me there. I wasn't going to get my hopes up—they didn't trust me to begin with, and this was just an excuse for them to get rid of me and not have to worry anymore.

Day turned into night, and I didn't hear any word from the Kausian. I knew it was going to be a failed attempt, but I had hoped I would hear from him. Since it sounded like everyone was going to go to sleep, I doubted I would hear anything tonight. I was getting tired, but I was not going to try to sleep. Why would I waste my last night sleeping when I could just sit here and contemplate what all had transpired over the past couple of weeks?

Chaos. Utter chaos.

Now that it was dark and people were beginning to retire for the night, I no longer heard people moving around in the distance. There was no one chatting while they ate dinner or while they worked. It was just me and the guards who had been changed out.

How long would these last few hours go? Would they be slow, or would they be quick?

Before I could contemplate these thoughts, I heard some noise outside the cell.

I stood up and tried to hear what was going on. I heard a few grunts and thumps, and suddenly Zach poked his head through the bars at the door.

"Zach! What are you doing?"

He grinned. "We are getting you out of here, of course."

I heard the metal click of the lock of the door, and it swung open.

I shook my head. "Why would you risk happiness for me?"

Zach laughed. "Living here would not have been happiness. We would have ended up being miserable. Besides, we have a planet to save."

I smiled a little. "While I doubt we will survive

trying to save the planet, I think those odds are better than waiting for morning."

He slapped my back. "There's the spirit. Now come—before someone notices."

Zach held out his hand, and I grabbed it and followed him.

CHAPTER IX

Ellie

Don't be suspicious. Don't be suspicious.

I kept repeating those words in my mind as I went to bed for the night—or at least acted like I was going to bed. Claude was in the cabin with me also retiring for the night. I wondered if he figured out Zach and I had hatched a plan already or not or if he was naive enough to think I would stand by and watch a friend be killed. Or he thought I would wait until the last minute to save him. I knew better than that—one had to act fast in case it backfired and you needed a second chance.

But I had a feeling a second chance wasn't going to happen in a place like this.

Once we left this cave, there was no turning back. We would never again have a home like this to go to and would be considered fugitives. It didn't matter—it wasn't as if we really had a home to begin with. The three of us had been troublemakers growing up, and some things never changed. We were lucky to be alive, if I were honest. We snuck into a lot of places we weren't supposed to go to when we were kids, and it wasn't as if other nations saw a Kausian child messing around and thought kids will be kids.

I felt bad for Claude and Edmund though—I didn't want to leave the two of them. Edmund was my brother, and while we did argue, I loved him more than anything. We were a lot alike—stubborn and a pain in the ass, which was probably why we got along so well. He taught me how to be strong.

As for Claude… well, I would feel bad for breaking his heart again. But if I left, he could finally move on knowing that I made the choice to leave. If I were honest though, I wanted to stay here with him because my brother was right—he was someone who would give me a stable home, and I wouldn't have to worry about him running off at the slightest of reasons.

The real question was whether we would go look for Cor once we got off these mountains. I had a feeling we wouldn't have to, and we would cross paths again.

"Are you all right?" Claude asked as he was about to blow out the candle.

I nodded. "Yeah, I'm fine."

"I'm really sorry, you know. We tried everything, but the council made up their mind."

I nodded. "I know. And I will have to live with the fact that I was the one who brought him into this mess."

"It's not your fault. It's Cor's fault for leaving him here. He should have known he would do something once he figured out it was the man who assassinated his mother."

He had a point there, but I didn't want to admit it. There was no time, however. Cor had to make a decision. We thought this would be best. I honestly didn't think Gabe would try to kill the man. He hadn't been very violent in the time we had known him, but anger and sadness would do that to a man —especially a man who had witnessed his mother's assassination.

"I know you are right, but it still shouldn't have happened—we should have been more careful."

He gently stroked my hand. "We can appeal to the council again in the morning, but I don't know if it will help. Thomas has been trying to convince them all day it was a mistake."

The Kausian who had killed Gabe's mother was named Thomas. I let out a breath. "We shall see in the morning then."

Claude kissed me gently and tucked himself into his bed. I lay there, listening to his breaths— waiting for it to be obvious that he was asleep. Claude always seemed like he was someone who fell asleep quickly—or at least he had been when we were younger. I remembered once I waited for him and my brother to fall asleep so I could sneak out with Cor. And by once, I meant quite a few times.

Claude's breathing slowed down, and I heard the faint sound of snoring. I slowly got up out of bed and made my way to the door. He didn't stir or anything but kept on snoring. I opened the door and slowly closed it behind me.

I half expected my brother to be standing outside the door, ready for me as I tried to rescue my friend, but he wasn't there like he had been a few times when I was younger. My lip twitched as I missed those days. He would scold me for a good hour and then would threaten Cor. Those were good times.

The plan was for Zach to sneak in and rescue Gabe and I would go and take out the guards at the gate. It was the only way out of here—that Cor and I found out the first couple of days we were here.

The cave was silent, and I did my best to not be heard. I had grabbed my shoes when I snuck out of the hut but decided not to put them on until I was closer to the gate so I could stay quiet while in my socks. The cave stayed pretty dry, surprisingly. My people knew how to make the best out of what they had.

I reached the doors before the gate that kept the cold air from coming into the cave. I quickly put on my boots, made sure it was just tranqs in my gun, and opened the door with my gun at the ready.

And the last person I ever thought would be standing there had his arms folded, giving me a judgmental look just like old times.

"Edmund. How did you…?"

"Like I don't know you, Ellie." He pinched the bridge of his nose. "Why must you always be a thorn in my side?"

I shook my head. "This isn't like old times, brother. I'm not running off for a good time—I'm saving my friend."

"I know… I just… After all this time, I thought perhaps we could be there for one another again—that I would have you back in my life."

"You still can. Help me—please. It's not just about Gabe but the entire world. We can stop a genocide from happening. We can bring peace back to Mu and perhaps the Kausians can finally find a home—"

"You know as well as I that won't happen. The seeds of discrimination were planted long ago. It would take a lot more than helping stop a war to undo all that they did."

I frowned. "You don't know that. When the truth comes out, perhaps people will realize their ways and come to appreciate us like they used to."

"What do you mean like they used to? The Kausians have been spat upon for generations."

"You are wrong—it has only been two generations. Before that we were revered. Byron's family caused some kind of event that made anyone fear us, and from that the prejudices came."

"Even if that was the case, that only shows me that the people wanted a reason to hate us. If they liked us so much, they should have questioned what happened and not turn on us so easily."

"Would you rather give up before finding out? Would you rather have all the other nations suffer the same fate as ours? I thought better of you, brother."

I could tell the words I had just said hurt him, but I didn't feel bad about saying them—they were true. The brother I knew wouldn't back down from a fight.

The door behind me opened, and I quickly turned around with my gun at the ready. It was Claude. I lowered my weapon.

"Ah—I see. You two hatched this plan," I said with a sigh. "What did you do with the guards that should be out here?"

Edmund answered, "I told them I couldn't sleep, and I would take watch for the night. They decided to just take a break and will be back around in a bit.

We don't have much time, so Ellie, please let's go back to the hut."

"No!" I yelled. "You don't understand, brother. I am not letting my friend die! Would you let me die if I were in his shoes?" I glanced at the both of them. They frowned.

"If you try anything and are caught, you will be killed. We are doing all this to protect you. Why can't you see that?" Edmund asked.

"Please, Ellie, listen to reason," Claude commented.

"You two listen to reason. I will keep fighting and trying to escape. I will do everything I can to protect a friend."

"Then what will you have us do? Just watch you leave? Worry about you the rest of my life?" Edmund asked. "I finally have you back in my life —we both have you back in our lives. I am not just going to watch you leave it all now."

"Then come with me. Both of you. With all five of us, we have a chance at saving Mu and destroying Jonathan once and for all. Don't you want to do it—not just to help the other nations— but to take revenge on what happened? To kill that son of a bitch once and for all?"

Claude glanced at Edmund. "She has a point—why don't we try taking them down?"

Edmund pinched the bridge of his nose. "Not you too."

"I'll be honest—I wanted to do something but have always been too scared. And I wanted to stay here in case Ellie ever came back. Now that she is here, I don't want to lose her. I want to help them with this—I want to help her. Let's do this. Let's get out of here and take the risk. The Edmund I used to know would have done just that."

"The Edmund you know died when he thought he lost his entire family. Now we have the responsibility of keeping our people safe."

"The only way we will be safe is if we stop this war," Claude said.

I smiled. With Claude on my side of the argument, the more likely we would be able to convince my brother. I turned to Edmund.

"Come on, brother. Where is your sense of adventure?"

He glanced between the two of us. "Fine, but that all rests on whether Zach will be able to break Gabe free."

"I know my friend—he will succeed."

CHAPTER X

Zach

I could do this—right?

I already knocked out the two guards that were at Gabe's cell, and Gabe was now free, but I worried that there were more people I would need to knock out, which wasn't necessarily something I wanted to do. These were my family, and I didn't want to hurt them.

Hopefully Ellie was successful in taking out the guards at the entrance to the cave. And hopefully her brother and Claude didn't notice we were gone. I doubted they would alert anyone of what we were doing and would simply try to take matters into their own hands rather than run the risk of the council wanting to execute us as well.

It was too late for that now. Once they realized what we had done, they'd want to kill us for sure.

They honestly couldn't blame us, could they? We had our reasons, and they had theirs. We were not only trying to save Gabe but also all the nations of Mu from Jonathan. These Kausians didn't want anything to do with the war since all the nations turned their backs on us, which was understandable. But neither Ellie nor I could turn our backs—not when we knew what we knew. We had gotten roped into the middle of it all, and we needed to enact our revenge.

"I didn't think you would come for me," Gabe whispered. "I thought for sure I was a dead man."

"We wouldn't leave a friend behind," I answered.

"But now you can't stay with your people—all because of me. I feel horrible—you shouldn't have to go through with this."

I shook my head. "We were never going to fully be welcomed here—not after the stunt Cor pulled, and because of some other things in the past. Even if you or Cor weren't here to begin with, Ellie and I wouldn't have truly belonged. Ellie doesn't like sitting still, and, well, I'm not fully Kausian. None of this is your fault, and while I do want to blame Cor, a lot of this isn't his fault either."

"No, it's my father's fault."

I was silent for a moment, because it was truly his father's fault all of this had happened—or, at least, his ancestors. But he wasn't then—he was his own person. "You can't choose your family, Gabe. None of us blame you for what your father has done. And we will find a way to stop him."

He nodded. "And I will do what I can to help."

As we rounded the corner, a man was standing with a knife in his hand. I quickly pulled my gun loaded with tranqs, and he held up his hands.

"Whoa, don't shoot—I was coming to do the same that you did."

I furrowed my brow and realized who the man was. "You're the person who Gabe tried to kill—why would you come help him?"

"I tried all day to convince the council to let him go, and they wouldn't listen. So I decided to take matters into my own hands and help free him. But I guess I'm a little late to the party."

Gabe nodded. "He speaks the truth—he came to the cell earlier today. I trust him."

I glanced between the two of them. I really didn't have time to sort all this. "Well, come on. All else fails, I can act like I am using you as a hostage."

"Oh, good idea. Take my knife then and let's go." He handed the knife to Gabe and followed us as we went to the gates.

And we found that find Ellie also had run into a problem—per the norm. Edmund and Claude were clearly not asleep. I supposed it wasn't the worst-case scenario, but I also didn't feel like fighting two people whom I considered family.

"Zach, why do you have that Kausian with you?" Ellie asked.

I nodded to Claude and Edmund. "And what about these two?"

"They are coming with us."

I glanced at the Kausian whom brought this entire mess. "Well, I don't think he is coming with us—although he did want to help Gabe out. I'm not sure what to do with him."

Ellie answered, "He can give the council a message. Tell them that they are cowards and should fight in this war to stop Mu from destroying themselves."

The Kausian raised an eyebrow. "You want me to tell them that?"

Ellie nodded and raised her tranq gun. "Yes. Now good night."

Without hesitating, she shot him, and he fell to the ground, passed out.

"Ellie!" Edmund exclaimed.

She put her gun away. "He's fine. It would be suspicious if we had hadn't knocked him out. Now we have someone who can tell the council what happened. They will have to decide on how to proceed with everything."

That was probably a harsh way to address the council, but I understood where Ellie was coming from. They were just hiding and making rash decisions to keep their secrets. Perhaps with all these people, we had a fighting chance against Jonathan.

But instead, it was probably just going to be the five of us. And perhaps Cor if we found him again.

I had a feeling he was going to make a last-ditch effort against Jonathan. While he did often run, he usually was self-destructive about it, and right now that would be the only way he could truly be destructive.

"Well then, shall we make our journey in the bitter cold before the guards come back?" Ellie asked.

We all nodded and headed out down the mountain.

It was dark and cold.

Luckily Claude and Edmund knew the quickest way back to the hut that we had made before finding out that the Kausians were out here. It wasn't the greatest shelter, but it was the best option for us while we waited for daylight, and we could grab some of the supplies we had left if any survived.

It took a couple of hours as it was dark out and we wanted to be careful with our footing. Not only that, but we also didn't want to use any lights in case someone might see us. Once we were no longer in view of the cave, Edmund turned on his flashlight.

Ellie smirked. "Oh, I see someone was ready to venture down the mountain. And here I thought you were against joining us."

Edmund huffed. "I brought it in case I had to chase after you. I wasn't planning on joining you."

"Mm-hmm."

I smiled a little. Hearing them bicker back and forth was going to be the best part of this trip. While to some it might have seemed annoying, to me it felt as if we could resume to some sort of normality. Although, I prayed they wouldn't start a full-blown fight again.

"Do you think they will send anyone after us?" Gabe asked as we kept moving forward toward our destination.

Claude shook his head. "Not at night, no. And even if they did, they didn't know where your camp was. Only Edmund and I went with Ellie to check it out. While it isn't completely out of the way from going down the mountain, it isn't really the direction they would assume we would go. Besides, since Edmund and I went with you both, they will be a bit less cautious about you three running and telling others where we are. They know we would never give up the secret location. But perhaps I am wrong. Only time will tell."

I didn't like the uncertainty in his statement, but it was the best we could do. Once we were off the mountain, we would be a bit safer—or, at least, safer from any Kausians following us. The moment we hit flat land, we would face the fact that our faces would be plastered everywhere.

Then a thought occurred to me—Claude's and Edmund's faces would be plastered everywhere, and they could get around a lot easier than we could. Well, easy for a Kausian.

Perhaps we could make this work and survive.

After a couple of hours, we reached the camp and all hustled inside. It was a bit cozy, but it would do until the night.

There was some wood in the makeshift furnace in the center of the room. It was clear that it had been used the night before.

"Seems Cor made it here just fine," I commented. "That or someone else is on this mountain."

"They would still be here if they had decided to make camp. Odds are that it was Cor. He would have needed somewhere to sleep and wait for daylight just like we do."

It was a good sign that Cor made it this far, but it also meant he probably took the supplies we were hoping to snatch before going down the mountain.

Ellie was able to start a fire though, and we gathered around for warmth. One didn't realize how cold Mu could get until they were up in the mountains like this. I couldn't imagine how harsh the winters got here.

And hopefully the rest of the Kausians didn't have to suffer another winter out here.

CHAPTER XI

Cor

I stood in the middle of the desolate landscape where Kaus once lay. I took a deep breath of the hot air and closed my eyes. I was drenched in sweat even after taking off most of my gear—a drastic contrast from the icy mountains. I may have been the autumn months, but it was still scorching hot.

Although it was all gone—although the bombs had destroyed everything that not even plants had grown back yet—I could still smell the campfires that would be held every couple of weeks. I could smell the bread my mother left on the windowsill to cool down. I could even smell the perfume that Ellie used to wear. She always used to smell like jasmine.

I opened my eyes to find nothing but dust and the two suns beating down on me. I always found myself here when everything in my life went to shit again. It was as if it set me in the right direction—as if it told me where to head.

But this time I didn't know where to go.

The Lyrans were the last ones left that hadn't begun a war of sorts with the humans. I had a feeling they wouldn't exactly trust some Kausian who claimed Byron and Jonathan were both scheming to destroy everything. I wasn't sure I would even believe it if I knew the truth. How could one family do so much damage to the world?

But I had to do something—I had to take down Jonathan if it was the last thing I did. If not for me, for everything on the mountain. For what they did to Gabe.

For the future Ellie and I could have had.

I glanced down at the ground and smiled. There was a small leaf sticking out of the sand. Perhaps life would find a way—things could grow again and be rebuilt. We just had to try.

Knowing I owed Ellie big time, I decided to head to the town we were at before we'd made a run for it. There were two horses I had to retrieve.

It was a bit out of the way from the Lyran Zone, but I needed some time to contemplate what I was going to do. First off, I wasn't sure which stalls they were in—however, there couldn't have been that many stalls one could leave their horses at in that tiny town. Secondly, there was the matter of paying them for the days that Ellie hadn't accounted for.

I had some money left in my pockets that I had kept just in case, but that was it. I could go to a hotel and get some money that way, but I didn't want to waste time or stay anywhere long enough to cause trouble. I would have to resort to the old tactics I used to use when I was a kid.

I was going to have to pickpocket some people.

It would have to be the right mark as well—ones that were clearly wealthy enough to be carrying a good amount of change and change that wouldn't be life-threatening if it were missing. It would also have to be people who weren't overcautious and notice what I was doing—especially if they were ones who would shoot first and ask questions later.

It took some time to get to the closest town, as Kaus was far from any of the towns. Luckily, there was a human town not too far from the border. It would take a few hours, but I would be able to reach it that night. I set off toward the town.

It was dark when I reached the town, which was perfect and meant it would be a bit easier to pickpocket someone. Glancing around, I found a man passed out outside a tavern. I swiped his cowboy hat and lowered it, so no one would notice my eyes. I made my way through the town, looking for the right mark to get some coin to pay for the horses and to pay for a night in a nice bed—or, at least, some sort of bed.

"Bingo," I whispered as I watched a drunk man in a nice suit stumble out of a bar. He was clearly dizzy and not sure where he was going. He began to fall forward. I caught him.

"Whoa, sir, do you need some help?"

He shook his head and shoved me away. "I don't need help. I am fine." He hiccuped and stumbled off down the street.

I pulled out the wallet I swiped. There was a large wad of cash in the wallet. Perfect. I stuck the cash in my pocket and dropped the wallet. Someone could find it and take it to the police, or the guy could have his ID stolen. It wasn't any of my business.

Figuring it would be best for me to get some sleep in a bed before figuring out how to get to the next town, I found one of the more run-down motels to stay at. I didn't want anyone to notice my existence. I would have to leave early in the morning just to be safe, but that was fine. I just needed a few hours to sleep to rest up before traveling.

And just prayed my face wasn't plastered on every motel wall like I feared it would be.

I walked into the first motel I found and glanced around. I didn't see my face or any other posters, in fact. This was the perfect seedy place I could camp out in.

"May I help you?" an old woman from behind the desk asked.

"Yes," I said, careful not to reveal my face—just in case. "Can I get one room?"

"That will be twenty a night."

I handed her the cash. "I only need one night. I will be out of there early morning."

"Leave the key in the room then," she said as she handed me the key. "Have a good night."

I thanked her and headed to the room number that was written on the key. I was on the second floor, which I preferred as then I didn't have to worry as much about someone breaking in through the window. It did happen every once in a while but definitely less frequently.

The room was quaint, which was perfectly fine. A bed was a bed. I pulled off the sheets to check for bugs. It was clean, surprisingly. I lay down on the bed and closed my eyes.

And I quickly fell asleep.

I woke to the old woman from the front desk standing over me. I jerked up and almost reached for my gun. She shook her head.

"You said you were going to be out by early morning. It is almost noon. If you don't leave right now, I am going to have to charge you for another night."

I blinked a few times. It was already noon? I grabbed for my things and wrapped my belt around my waist.

"I'll be out. Just give me a second."

"You are lucky you are pretty—even with those golden eyes of yours."

I glanced at her. She didn't seem as if she had any negative intentions, but I learned not to assume anyone was that nice. I finished grabbing the gear I had from the mountains and put my hat back on.

"Good day, ma'am."

She just huffed a response and began ripping the sheets off the bed. I left the room and rubbed my eyes. I couldn't believe I slept in for that long. That had been a great mistake. I just hoped the man didn't report me stealing his wallet. I would have to keep my head down and stay away from any officers, not that I wasn't going to already. Jonathan might have alerted every town of my identity—even ones on the outskirts like this.

I hurried to the carriage services. Luckily this town had one, and I went straight to the man in charge and pointed at the map.

"What will it cost for me to get to here?" I asked.

"Thirty-five."

I put the cash on the table and added an extra ten. "Get me there quickly?"

He nodded as he called out to one of the younger hands. The teen who had to have been younger than Gabe hurried off to grab a horse and ready him. I waited, glancing down the street in fear that officers were, in fact, looking for me, but there were none. I hated living in fear like this— especially when everything was fine. It made it all the worse.

I didn't want to live in constant fear any longer.

The teen got the carriage ready and brought it around front. He apparently was also going to be my driver. I just hoped we got there in one piece.

A few hours went by, and everything went smoothly, which I wasn't used to. I had half expected bandits to try to rob us at some point. As we entered the town, I felt my heart race.

He wouldn't think we would come back here, would he?

Odds were that Jonathan wouldn't think we would be so stupid and that we were no longer a threat. I would just have to keep my cool and not get into any trouble.

It was a stupid idea to come back here, but I owed Ellie.

The carriage got through the gates, and the driver

turned back to me. "Where to, sir?"

Sir? Ugh, this kid made me feel older than I really was. "To the stables."

CHAPTER XII

Gabe

These people risked their lives for me.

I still didn't know how I felt about it all. They could have been happy staying in the settlement— they could have lived happily ever after, but I had ruined it all for them.

No. They also want to fight Jonathan. They had more than one reason to leave. I just happened to also need saving.

I needed to remember there was more at stake

than just my life. We had to stop this all-out war from happening and save all the nations from destruction. Even if the humans won this war, which my father believed would happen due to generations of manipulation and setup, many humans would die. But he didn't care about them— they were just collateral damage.

It was disgusting.

While I knew I was a product of this madness, and that I didn't choose to be born in this family, I still wanted to help end it all. It was my birthright. It would be the only way to stop this generational trauma. Then, perhaps, I could move on with my life. Perhaps we could all move on with our lives.

But where would we all go after that? Would we stay together, or would we slowly move apart?

Those were worries for another day. First, we needed to defeat Jonathan and then we could go from there.

The light began to shine, and we gathered what supplies were left in the hut. Cor had taken a lot of it, which made sense since he was alone and didn't think we would be coming here anytime soon. He probably figured we would live happily ever after without him.

I couldn't wait to give him a piece of my mind.

"Once we get down the mountain, where do you want to head to first?" Edmund asked. "We might want to go a different way depending on which nation you all wanted to go to."

"The only nation that the Human Zone hasn't declared war on is the Lyran Zone. Our best bet is to go there," Ellie said with a sigh. "Although I'm not sure how much has happened since we left even if it hasn't been that long."

Edmund nodded. "There are two ways to get to the Lyran Zone. We can either get out of the cold quicker and travel through the ruins or we can go straight down through the mountains, but we will have to make camp in the cold."

"So, either we make camp in the heat or in the freezing cold?" Zach asked. "Those are great choices."

"We might be able to make it to a settlement on the edge of Kaus, but it will be in the Human Zone," Claude added.

Ellie frowned. "We would be risking running into trouble if we do that."

"But we do need supplies," Edmund added. "If the three of you stay out of sight and Claude and I do all the taking and negotiating, we should be fine."

"They might be on the lookout for any Kaus, not just us."

Edmund shrugged. "Is that any different from every other day of our lives?"

Ellie laughed ironically. "That's a fair point. Then let's do that. Does that sound good with everyone else?"

We all nodded in unison.

Ellie clapped her hands together. "All right. Let's get ready for the freezing cold and then the extreme heat."

The walk down the mountain wasn't as treacherous as I thought. It was much easier since it was light out compared to the night before. We stayed quiet and listened for anyone who might be trying to follow us but heard nothing. It was clear that they didn't want to send people after us as the mountain was vast. That, or Ellie's comment got to them. Perhaps they wanted us to make a run for it so they didn't have blood their hands.

It took a few hours, but we made it down the mountain. How quickly Edmund and Claude were able to venture down through the snow made it clear that threat of this area was not knowing where to go. I imagined a lot of people got lost throughout these mountains.

Just as Ellie said, once we got down the mountain and ventured a little into the desert, it got extremely hot. We all quickly took off our winter gear. The suns were brutal, and I couldn't imagine living in an environment like this.

I wanted to make a comment, but as I glanced at the others, I could tell they didn't want to talk. Their faces were full of deep sadness. This was their home, and while I didn't know what it looked like before the attack, I had a feeling it wasn't just all dust—even with this heat.

And this was what Jonathan had planned for all the nations.

Except for the Sirians. He just wanted them to stay in the water, which I had a feeling he was successful in doing. Sirians already didn't like outsiders, and many of them never left the water. They wanted any excuse to close the border to the city.

I wondered once we won this war—if we won this war—whether I could convince them what happened and to open the gates or if they still thought I was the one who killed my own mother. My sister knew the truth, and hopefully with time, she would stand up for what was right and help reestablish order—but she was young, and I feared someone would manipulate her memories. My father threatened he would do just that.

We had to stop him.

It took a couple of hours, but we were able to finally cross through Kaus and get to the Human Zone. The town on the border was small with only a few buildings with houses on the outskirts. Ellie, Zach, and I kept our heads down outside as Claude and Edmund went to secure a room. After a few minutes, they reappeared.

Edmund dangled two sets of keys in his hands. "We got a couple of rooms. Also, it sounds like Cor was here earlier today."

My eyes widened. "How do you know that?"

"The old lady at the front desk made a comment that she saw someone with similar eyes this morning," Claude said as he watched Ellie's reaction. Her eyes widened in surprise, but she didn't say a word. "Or, at least, I assume it was Cor. It could have been another Kausian."

"Which way did he go?" I asked. "Did she say?"

Edmund shook his head. "We didn't ask. There are quite a few places he could have headed to from here. Finding him would be like finding a needle in a haystack. We should focus on getting supplies and some rest and head to the Lyran Zone in the morning."

Ellie nodded. "I agree. He could be anywhere by now. It's best if we focus on our mission. Now the three of us should go to the room and wait while Edmund and Claude get supplies."

"Right." Claude let out a breath. It was clear he wished Ellie could go with us. "Let's go, Edmund."

The two of them left, and I followed Ellie and Zach as we headed to our room. It was quaint but clean and, more importantly, warmer than the mountain had been. I sat on the bed and let out a deep breath.

"Don't get too comfortable," Ellie commented as she opened the curtains a crack and peered outside. "We need to be on guard in case this town has wanted posters."

"I haven't seen any," Zach said as he too collapsed on the bed. "And if Cor came through here unscathed, then we should be fine."

"That's assuming he didn't get arrested or kidnapped," Ellie added. "Although I doubt the woman at the front desk would make a comment if that had been the case."

"She could have just not witnessed the arrest," Zach retorted. "But Cor is pretty slippery and probably is off doing whatever by now."

"Probably." Ellie sighed.

"You think he's fine then?" I asked, the worry apparent in my voice.

"As fine as he can be." Ellie stepped back from the window. "We'll probably run into him at some point, so I wouldn't worry. Our fates are intertwined. It would be strange if we didn't run into him later."

I smiled a little. "You believe in fate, Ellie?"

She shrugged. "I think we are meant to stop Jonathan. Why else would we have been connected to all the attacks? Sure, Byron wanted to torment us all, but I think there is more to that. I think we'll figure out a way to stop him or die trying."

"I agree," Zach said. "While I would have liked to live a calm life with the Kausians on the mountain, it didn't feel right. We are meant to do something."

Ellie smiled as she also jumped on the bed. "And who knows? Maybe our names will go down in history—whether it be better or for worse."

CHAPTER XIII

Ellie

I hated always being paranoid someone was going to either arrest me or kill me.

It was a feeling I had to live with my entire life. Why couldn't I live freely, whatever that meant? I didn't know what it was like not to have to look over my shoulder. Would the knot that lived in my stomach cease to exist? Or was the damage done and no matter what we did it would always be there?

The first sun was beginning to set, and I began to worry for Claude and Edmund. I figured they would be back by now, but perhaps they had trouble finding everything they needed. I bit at my nails as I peeked through the blinds again.

"They are fine," Zach commented. "They aren't wanted."

"All Kausians are wanted. It's whether how bad they are wanted and how much a person wants money."

"The small towns don't usually deal with stuff like that—we are fine."

I nodded, but I still worried. If anything happened to my brother and Claude after all this time, I would be devastated.

But I might have to face that fact if things went south during the battle that was inevitable.

I tried not to worry about that. I would face that issue when it happened. There was no use thinking about things that haven't been determined. We would survive—we always did.

I saw movement coming this way, and I put my hand on the holster until I noticed it was my brother and Claude. The door opened, and I took my hand away from my gun.

Their arms were filled with stuff, and they were both wearing wide-brimmed hats. Claude's curly dark hair stuck out from underneath the hat, and it made me smile a little. He glanced at me and saw my grin.

"What are you smiling at?"

I wrapped my arms around him. "Just smiling at how adorable you are in this hat."

I gave him a kiss on the lips.

"Don't distract him and make him drop his bags —some of that is fragile." My brother sighed.

I stepped away. "Oh? What would be fragile?"

"Jams, honey, those sorts of things," Claude explained as he set it down. "And don't worry, we got you all some hats and wraps to cover your faces as much as possible without sticking out like a sore thumb as well."

"Did you see your faces plastered anywhere?" Zach asked.

They both shook their heads.

Edmund answered, "No—seems this town was too small for anyone to care."

While that was a relief, I had my doubts about it all. What if it was just a setup? What if we were walking into some trap? We had done so before, and I doubted that was the last time.

Or maybe Jonathan really thought we would never show our faces again.

Or maybe Edmund was right and this was such a small town that Jonathan didn't bother. It wasn't as if we could do much harm here, and he knew the locals wouldn't warm up to us anytime soon. We needed to leave in the morning before people noticed a group of Kausians were here and decided to drive us out of town with pitchforks and torches.

It wouldn't be the first time.

"Did anyone seem suspicious?" Gabe asked.

Edmund chuckled. "I think we are the ones who appear suspicious. But if you mean looks that aren't quite normal for what we are used to, no—no one seemed suspicious."

Gabe nodded. "That's good, I guess."

"As good as it can be for the likes of us." I sighed. "Nothing exciting happened here. Zach and Gabe were able to get a shower in. I was just about to take one myself, then you two can take a turn."

"Sounds good. We got some clothes to change into. We can also do a wash and hang them to dry," Edmund said and then pointed at Claude. "No."

I rolled my eyes as Claude looked all defensive

and beet red. "I wasn't—ugh."

Closing the door to the bathroom behind me, I took a long breath and let it out slowly. That would have been something Cor would have suggested—not Claude.

We all took our showers and washed our clothes before the second sun had set. We left the clothes in the bathroom to dry since we didn't want anyone swiping them in the night. It was warm enough in the hotel room for them to dry by the time morning came.

Zach and I shared a bed while my brother and Claude took the other bed and Gabe slept on the couch. The couch, to be honest, appeared comfier than the hard beds, but I wasn't going to complain. We were all warm, and our stomachs were filled, and that was the most any of us could ask for. Then, in the morning, we would begin our venture toward the Lyran Zone.

The Lyran Zone wasn't far from where we were at that moment—it was just going to be a bit of a walk unless we gathered some horses.

"Hey, Zach," I whispered.

"What is it?" he asked in a whisper.

"Do you think we can go get Kevin and Charlotte?"

I could hear him let out a breath. "It's too much of a risk. They are in the town that Jonathan lives in. Besides—it is a bit out of the way, isn't it?"

"Yeah, I know. I just miss them."

"I do too. Once all this is over, or at least if we get the chance, we will get them back. I promise."

He squeezed my hand, and I tried not to let tears form in my eyes. They were like family to us—we didn't go anywhere without them. If anything happened to them, I would be devastated.

The night came and went, and I was able to get some sleep, but too many what-ifs filled my mind. Were we going to make it to the Lyran Zone? Were they going to believe us? Or had Jonathan beat us to it? Were Kevin and Charlotte all right?

We gathered all our things and left the moment the suns were in the sky. As we closed the hotel door behind us, the old woman appeared.

"Seems you weren't like that other one who slept through morning and into the afternoon."

Yeah—that sounded like Cor.

I knew I shouldn't talk to her since we didn't want to take more time here than need be, but I couldn't help myself. "Was this person about this tall and has short blond hair?"

She nodded. "Yup. And he had golden eyes just like you lot."

I noticed Claude's frown, but I ignored it. At the end of the day, Cor was still my friend. He couldn't be jealous of that. "Do you know which way he went?"

She shook her head. "Nope. He ran the moment I woke him. I don't like to get into my customers' business either—things run more smoothly that way."

I figured as much. "Thank you, ma'am. Have a great day."

"Yeah, yeah. You all better get out of here. Rumors have been spreading already. Our town is small, and we don't like trouble."

Claude put his arm around me. "Don't worry. We are leaving. Thank you again."

We had about a two-day hike to Kiron—the capital of the Lyran Zone. It seemed that Claude and Edmund had bought a tent—not wanting to stay in a town if we didn't have to. That was probably the safest plan of action.

We stepped outside of the town, and I glanced

north toward where Kaus once stood. We would bring our home back if it was the last thing we did.

CHAPTER XIV

Zach

Why must walking take so long?

We couldn't afford to purchase enough horses for all five of us, and stealing them was out of the question. While we did steal a couple from Jonathan, that was different. In a small town like this, the theft would be noticed, and someone could be out a lot of money, if not their livelihood. They could also be close pets, just like Ellie's and ours had been. We may have been outlaws, but we weren't monsters.

While I wanted to go back for Charlotte and Kevin, it wasn't possible at the moment. The town they were being held in was the opposite direction from where we needed to go, and it was too risky. It was the town Jonathan lived in, and it was possible we might run into him or one of his guards. We would go back for them the first chance we had, however. But I had no idea when that would be.

And we just had to pray they weren't sold by then.

Ellie gave them a lot of money, so odds were they hadn't been sold yet. But the more time that went by, the more likely they would be sold.

I tried not to think about it.

Long story short, we were walking and would be walking for two, maybe three, days. At least we wouldn't be walking up a mountain, and it would be mostly a leveled hike. This area was mainly plains or forests rather than desert and snow, so I couldn't really complain. Even though it was warm out, it was still pretty cool compared to the Kausian desert we had just traveled through. While walking through where our town once stood was quite cumbersome yesterday, I had to admit even where there was a town and some plant life, it had always been that hot. We managed though. We always did.

"Hey, Ellie." I smiled.

"I know what you are going to say, and I am not playing," she replied.

I frowned playfully, "Hey, that's no fun. We used to play all the time."

She shook her head. "No, you used to play, and I would have to humor you."

I pouted. "You are so mean."

"Play what?" Gabe asked.

I grinned. "Have you played I, Spy?"

He cocked his head. "No, what is it?"

"It's a game where I give you clues of what I see and then you have to guess. It's pretty simple."

"Seems like fun." Gabe smiled. "I'll play."

"Okay! I spy something… green."

Ellie let out a sigh as her brother laughed. "Some things never change, Zach. I knew what you were going to pick before you even said anything."

"Shh," I said. "You will ruin it for him."

"Um." Gabe glanced around. "Grass?"

"Nope!" I grinned ear to ear. "Try again."

Gabe glanced around. "I guess a tree?"

I held up a finger. "Ah, but which tree?"

Gabe realized the horror of this game. "There are trees all over. I have to figure out which one?"

Ellie chimed in. "Now you understand why we don't want to play this game with him. He always picks something there is a lot of. It takes forever, and he just stands there and grins."

I put my hands on my hips in triumph. "Which is why I always win."

Ellie rolled her eyes and pointed. "It's that one."

I frowned. "How did you know?"

"I know you too well, Zach. And I also know how to watch someone's eyes. It's yours, and a lot of other people's, tell."

"Some things never change." Edmund laughed. "Ellie was always good at games. She can read someone like a book."

"Well, I spy something beautiful," Claude commented.

I glanced at Ellie, who I found blushing. I answered, "Is it Gabe?"

Gabe smiled. "Aww, you think I'm beautiful, Zach?"

It was my turn to blush. "I was just—er—I mean, you aren't bad to look at."

Ellie chimed in. "You are definitely one of the more handsome marks we have had, Gabe."

"I feel like that was a compliment. Somewhere in there at least." Gabe let out a sigh. "That seems like so long ago, but it has barely been a month."

"I know," I added. "A lot has happened in a month. I don't think any of us have actually processed it all yet."

"And we don't have time too," Ellie added. "Not until we stop Jonathan."

I nodded. "Right. However that is going to work."

"Stuff like this takes a long while to process," Edmund added. "It takes a long while to even sink in. I don't think I broke down crying until a month after the destruction of Kaus. It was just so… horrific that our bodies didn't know what to do."

Claude nodded in agreement. "And it took a while to realize who was really gone. There was hope that other people made it out, but reality sunk in, and we knew the truth." He turned to Ellie and I. "Except I suppose we were wrong for you two. I never could have imagined that the two of you were still alive after all this time."

"And we could never have imagined that a whole

group of Kausians escaped to the mountains," Ellie added. "I'm glad we found the two of you. It gives me hope that perhaps some we still have some good luck on our side."

The somber thought left us quiet for a while. I kept an ear out, as I assumed others did, for any other people on this trail. While there was a main road that went toward the different Lyran cities, we were taking more of a hiking path that bypassed the smaller cities and went straight to the capital. Odds were that there could be bandits on this trail, and we had to stay alert.

Hours went by, and I was starting to get hungry, but I didn't want to say anything. I had a feeling hunger would overcome them soon enough as well.

We came to a patch of grass under a few trees. Ellie nodded toward it. "We can stop there to rest and get some food."

My stomach gurgled in happiness. I wasn't sure if anyone else heard it, but I saw Gabe smile a little.

Claude and Edmund opened the packs they had put together and put them down on the ground for us to pass around. I grabbed a piece of bread and put some jam and honey on it.

Nothing tasted better than fresh bread with jam and honey. I smiled as I scarfed it down and waited for the others to take their share.

"Don't eat all of it," Ellie commented. "We have tomorrow to travel as well."

"I know, I know. I was going to pace myself after the first piece."

We continued to eat, talking about minor things like the last time we all had strawberries or how we missed Ellie and Edmund's mom's baking. While we cherished those memories and they were happy times, there was a bit of a sadness in our voices. Everything had been taken from us so quickly—it wasn't fair.

As we sat there and ate our food, we heard the sound of hooves coming our way. We were all quick to grab our guns, ready to defend ourselves if need be.

Then, as the figures rounded the corner, I couldn't believe my eyes.

"Charlotte?" I whispered as Ellie bolted up and ran toward the figures.

There, on the trail, was Cor with our two horses. He grinned as Ellie ran toward him with her arms open. Cor opened his arms as Ellie ran straight past him and hugged her horse.

I saw the smug look on Claude's face.

Getting up, I hurried over to Charlotte. She huffed and stomped her front hoof. "I know, I know —we shouldn't have left you, but you wouldn't have been able to go where we went—it was too cold, and we didn't have food for you. You were safer at the stables."

She stomped again. I petted her and kissed the side of her face.

"I missed you, my beautiful girl."

Ellie finished hugging Kevin and turned to Cor. "How? Why?"

Cor shrugged. "I remembered you said you left your horses in the stable in the town Jonathan was in. I decided going to get them was the least I could do—after all, you left them there to rescue me."

"How did you find us?" I asked as Gabe made his way over to us.

"Accident, to be honest. I was just heading to the Lyran Zone and saw these trees and figured I would take a break. I had no idea you were over here."

Gabe stepped up to Cor, and Ellie and I exchanged glances. This was definitely awkward.

"Gabe, I'm—"

Gabe pulled back his fist and punched Cor straight in the jaw. Cor lost his balance and went down on one knee.

"You left me! I was almost executed!"

Cor turned to him. "What?"

"The Kausian that killed my mother was there, and all I saw was red! I tried to kill him and was caught. Then they were going to execute me! These people had to come to my rescue, and now they can't go back all because you ran!"

Standing back up, Cor responded, "If I didn't run, I would have been killed immediately."

"You left me! You didn't say goodbye—you didn't expect to see me again! How could you do that?"

Cor opened his mouth and closed it again. While I understood why Cor ran, I understood how betrayed Gabe felt. He was an outsider no matter where he went, and Cor had been the only one who accepted him. Of course he was going to feel betrayed.

"I'm sorry. I had to act fast, but I should have gone looking for you. We should have escaped together, then none of this would have happened. I made a poor decision, but I want to make it right.

We can save Mu once and for all, and then we can live happily ever after—what do you say?"

I glanced at Ellie, who I saw frown a little. She hid it well as she didn't want Claude to notice. He was still under the tree and couldn't hear us, so I doubt he could.

"Do you have any food?" Ellie asked. "We are just finishing up lunch."

He glanced over at Claude and Edmund. "Yeah, I have my own stuff. I doubt your boyfriend would appreciate me taking his things."

Ellie punched him in the shoulder and headed back to the picnic we had going. I had to hand it to those two—they sure knew how to make life more complicated.

CHAPTER XV

Cor

I sat awake staring at the fire, contemplating what to do next.

I didn't expect to run into Gabe and the others so quickly—if at all. I figured I would at least get to save the day first and then could go back and tell them they were free to live down here, out of the mountains. I knew going back might cost my life, but at least I could die feelings as if I had fixed what I could, even if it would never restore everything. But instead, they were here, figuring out a way to convince the Lyrans to not trust Jonathan.

And they brought Claude and Edmund with them. Even if I imagined running into Gabe, Zach, and Ellie, I never would have imagined they brought those two with them. Edmund and Claude had made a life for themselves among the Kausians —why would they risk all that to come down here?

No, I knew why. Because of Ellie.

I felt a sting in my heart. Claude wasn't going to let Ellie go, not that it mattered since Ellie could make her own decisions. But he has been in love with her since we were all kids, and he wasn't a screw-up like I was. He could provide Ellie with everything she could ever need, whereas I would always have to look behind my back, even after this was over. Not to mention I had left her behind multiple times.

And there was no way the Kausians would ever accept me as one of their own again.

Then Edmund tagged along since he wanted to protect his sister. He was always like that— meddling in when I had everything covered. Well, usually. He was overprotected, to say the least. He probably had every right to be with me hanging around, but that didn't mean I liked it.

Besides Gabe telling me that he was almost executed, no one spoke about what happened after I felt and why exactly they ran away. I had a feeling I knew why—they all found out about the crimes I had committed.

It wasn't just giving the codes to Byron. No, they knew about my days bounty hunting. They didn't say it, but since neither Claude nor Edmund was looking at me, that had to be it. Otherwise, they would have been giving me an earful.

Which made sitting much, much worse.

They knew they needed me though. They knew more people on our side meant we were more likely to take Jonathan down. I had a feeling, though, after all this was over, there would be a lot of people who wanted to see me in jail, if not worse.

No, they would want me dead.

And now I couldn't try to make it right by saving the day. Now, it would be them, and I would just have my revenge taken away from me yet again. It wasn't fair—I should be the one to kill Jonathan. I had to be the one. Or else, everything I had done would be all for nothing.

I tried not to think about that and focus on the present. Right now, we had to convince the Lyrans that Jonathan was going to start a war, and they had to

Glancing over at Ellie, I found she and Claude were snuggled up together. I knew I shouldn't be jealous, as Gabe was next to me and leaning his head against my shoulder, but I couldn't help it. I had loved her for so long, just as Claude had. He had always been there, waiting for the right moment… I never imagined it would be under these circumstances, especially since I thought he was dead all this time.

Then there was the fact that Edmund would do anything he could to make sure Ellie ended up with him rather than me.

And that wasn't my fear or insecurities talking either. He had said that to my face more than once. Quite often actually. Usually every time we snuck back to her house late at night or were brought back to Kaus by some officers. Especially when we were brought back by some officers.

The memories brought a smile to my lips. Those days of being a worry-free teen were long gone.

Now we were sitting here with the fate of the entire world on our backs. Never in my wildest dreams did I think I would end up in this situation. Not with all the chaos we had brought upon the world just as children.

But it was that lack of confidence—that need to prove to him I was worthy—that made me want to go to a human university. I should have known it wasn't possible—I should have known that it would end up in failure. I would never be lucky enough to lead a happy life. I was born without luck in my life.

"We should reach the capital tomorrow. Any ideas how we should try to convince the president of the Lyrans?" Edmund asked.

We were all silent. None of us knew how we were going to do it. I didn't even know if it would be possible. Why would a Lyran believe a bunch of Kausians that were all wanted for one thing or another.

"Tell the truth," Gabe said. "I could tell him who I am and what Byron and Jonathan did."

"He might turn you in to the Sirians," Ellie commented.

Gabe shrugged. "At this point, anyone could. I'm

sure all our faces are on wanted posters. I think being honest will be the only way to win them over."

I nodded. "While it will be risky, I think that might be the best option. He will be used to be people lying to him—he is a politician after all. Honestly will a surprise that might make him listen. What do you all think?"

Everyone nodded. We were going all in. I just prayed to the goddess that it worked.

We all took turns sleeping and keeping watch until morning. We still had almost a full day of walking before we got to the capital. I was glad that it wasn't as hot out here as it had been in the Human Zone the day before, and there was plenty of tree cover. It was still a lot of walking, but at least we had two horses to use to carry our belongings. That always made a huge difference. And if any of us got too tired, we could ride one of the horses.

The day went by without a hitch, which surprised me. I was so used to having everything go wrong every step of the way that I had expected bandits to capture us or a bunch of officers coming by and recognizing us.

We reached the Lyran gates, and I noticed Ellie and Zach glance at one another.

I let out a sigh. "What is it?" I asked.

"Well… this was where Byron hired us, and there was a sort of… situation before we left town. I forgot that really wasn't that long ago, and I'm not sure if we will be recognized," Ellie answered.

"What sort of… Oh." Then I remembered—Krax had hired me to kill the two of them due to an incident involving them and some Silurians. Apparently they had killed a few in a bar brawl, but I knew that wasn't the case. Bullets were too expensive for them to waste on some Silurians in a bar.

"Look at it this way," I went on. "All our faces could be recognized by anyone at any time. It will be the same outcome either way."

"I guess you have a point." She sighed. "We could be walking into all sorts of traps."

She wasn't wrong there. While it really wasn't much time we had been gone, it was enough for Jonathan to pull strings. They already had woven their web of lies—but we were people who he hadn't planned for. We were wild cards.

The guards let us in without any problems, which

surprised all of us. We made our way through town, watching for any signs of trouble, but most people paid us no mind. We all kept our hats low, careful to reveal our eyes to any passerby—especially if they looked like they could be bounty hunters or officers.

After traveling through the city, we came upon the capitol building. It was nothing fancy—in fact, I was pretty sure Jonathan and Byron's estate was larger—but it was still grand compared to the buildings around it.

It was all or nothing now.

Edmund turned to us. "We will go in first and ask to see the president. Odds are, they aren't going to let us in. Keep an eye out for any other ways in or which way you think he leaves. We could catch him on his way out."

We all nodded, and both Edmund and Claude entered the building. The four of us began searching around the building discreetly, but there were no easy access points. After a few moments, we all ended up back at the front.

Claude and Edmund hadn't come out of the building yet. We waited for them to see if they had any luck, but before we could find out, a voice spoke from behind us.

"Well, well. What do we have here?"

CHAPTER XVI

Gabe

My entire body froze, and my heart began to race. Everything in front of me turned blurry, and all I could see was red.

My father was behind us. He was here. He was going to stop us. We were going to fail before we even started. This wasn't fair—none of this was fair.

Finally able to move, I turned to face my father.

He grinned as he looked down at me, examining

my state of being. "Gabriel, I see you survived the poison. What a relief. I was truly worried. But you do look worse for wear—have you lost a few pounds?"

I couldn't speak—it felt as if I were a statue. And the fact that Zach, Ellie, and Cor hadn't spoken meant they felt the same as I did. Everything had been going so smoothly—we should have known he would show up. Byron and my father always showed up at the worst possible moment—the moment we had some hope in our hearts.

"Aren't you going to say how much you missed your father? Where have you been?" He glanced up at Cor and the others. "I see you are still with these Kausians. You should really reconsider—they are a bad batch of people."

Ellie spat at him just as the soldiers surrounded all of us. One of the soldiers smacked her. She hit the ground.

"Stop it!" I yelled.

"Ah, so you can talk. I worried that the poison might have made you mute. Now let me guess why you are here. To speak to the Lyran president, am I right?" Jonathan asked.

I didn't like where this was going. None of us

answered him.

Jonathan laughed. "Well, today is your lucky day! I have a meeting with him shortly. Why don't we all go in and talk to him together?"

He placed his arm on my shoulder, and it felt as if he were staring right through me. "That is, if you want these three to live."

So he still thought it was just us—he didn't know about Claude and Edmund. They were still in the building—we wouldn't have to keep those two safe from him. Then perhaps they could rescue us, depending on how this conversation would end.

"You bastard." Ellie glared at Jonathan. "You've waiting for us this entire time, haven't you?"

He turned to her. "I knew you would try to pull something, so I decided to have my men keep an eye out for you here. It took you some time to make it here—I can only imagine where you have been in the meantime. I was growing impatient and decided to finish my plan without you. But alas, you showed just in time. Now, with my son, I will be able to convince the Lyran governor to hand over control to me in order for us to stop a full-blown war from starting."

I shook my head. "As if I will help you—there is

no way I will go along with what you say."

My father nodded to one of his henchmen, and the henchman punched Cor straight in the stomach. He fell to his knees, grabbing at his stomach.

"No!" I yelled out. "Stop it!"

Jonathan grinned. "All you need to do is help me convince the Lyrans to sign this treaty, and I will let you and your little friends go. How does that sound?"

I knew he wasn't telling the truth—I knew there would be no way any of us were walking out of this alive—but if I stood up to him now, then he would kill one of them on the spot.

I shook my head. "You, you are lying—you won't let them go after all of this."

"Gabriel, you have my word."

"That means nothing to me."

My father let out a sigh. "We can either do this the easy way or the hard way. You can agree to my deal and, believe me, it won't get any better than what I have offered—or you can stand there and watch as my men break their limbs one at a time. Starting with Cor."

He gestured to his men who shoved Cor down and laid out his arm.

"No!" I yelled out. "Fine—I will help you. Just promise me they will walk free after the treaty is signed."

"Don't do it, Gabe!" Cor yelled. "He won't keep his word! He's a liar."

I knew Cor was right, but I couldn't risk it. Perhaps while my father talks to the Lyran leader, I can do something to stop it all—even if it will cost me my life.

Jonathan put his hand on my shoulder. "You have yourself a deal."

He nodded to the henchmen, who began to drag Ellie, Zach, and Cor away. Ellie appeared as if she wanted to yell something, but she glanced over to the other side of Jonathan and held her tongue. I moved my gaze casually to where she was looking to find Claude and Edmund turning around and acting as if they were simply other citizens.

They knew we were being captured. I prayed to the goddess that they would follow Ellie and the others and help them to escape. That meant I would just have to buy them all some time.

But I also couldn't act like I was giving in so easily or else he might think something was up.

Then again, he and Byron thought I was a

pushover—a wimp—that would easily give in to any command. They had planned on this since my birth.

It was sickening to think I was only born so this man could try to take over the world and commit mass genocide. He had used my mother and me just to get into the Sirian Zone. I didn't know if they had always planned on using a Kausian to appear like me to kill my mother or if that was Byron trying to thwart my father's plans or if he had no idea what my father's plans were. It didn't seem like the two of them agreed to how to take over the world, or perhaps neither of them wanted to share the power. Either way, I didn't want anything to do with any of it.

My father and a couple of his guards escorted me inside the capitol building. The Lyrans were a proud race that appeared catlike. There were many different appearances of Lyrans, including ones with large manes, short fur, and all sorts of coloring. Their land was situated in an area with many precious gems and crystals; so much of the interior of the capitol building was decorated as such. There were carvings of precious leaders, battles they had won, pillars that were two stories tall.

It was all a bit much.

We went up to the receptionist desk, and I kept quiet as my father spoke. "Hello, I am Jonathan Pickett. Governor Riazusryz is expecting me."

The receptionist picked up her phone that probably went straight to the governor and started speaking. "Sir, there is a man by the name of Jonathan Pickett here to see you. Mm-hmm. Sure, I will send him up." She hung up the phone and turned to us. "He will see you now. Please follow these men—they will show you the way."

Jonathan nodded. "Thank you, ma'am."

She also nodded and went back to her work as my father nudged me to follow the guard. The guard led us up the stairs and down the hall to the farthest door on the right. He opened the door, and there stood a large Lyran with a dark mane and golden face. His piercing green eyes watched us as we stepped in.

"Jonathan Pickett," the governor said as he stood. "Long time, no see."

He reached out a hand that Jonathan shook. "Yes, it has been quite a while since I attended any of my brother's soirees. He was always the more social butterfly compared to me."

"Yes, that he was. I am sorry to hear about his death. It was truly a shock to all of us."

Did he know that it was the man in front of him that had killed Byron? Before I could say anything, my father responded.

"Yes, that is actually what I wanted to talk to you about. It seems that it was a Lyran that murdered my brother."

I had to hold back my laugh. Did Jonathan really believe Riazusryz would buy such an accusation?

Riazusryz furrowed his brow. "I don't understand —my people loved Byron. None of them would commit this kind of act."

"My son here and I witnessed it all. He claimed to be working under your command."

I watched as the governor tried to piece together the information he was given. He shook his head. "I can't believe that. Byron and I were close—I would never have betrayed him. I want to see this Lyran you speak of. You must have been mistaken."

"I am afraid he got away during the chaos that happened. We chased him into the wilderness but eventually lost him. I do, however, have footage of the act if you would like to see."

Riazusryz frowned. "I suppose I must. Give it here."

My father handed him the video drive, and Riazusryz placed it into the computer. A screen appeared from his desk, and the next thing I knew, I was watching footage from the house where my father had killed Byron—only it was not footage from what actually happened. My father must have put together an entire play just for this moment.

He and Byron were a lot alike.

After the video of a Lyran killing Byron was over, the governor leaned back in his chair in defeat. He fiddled with his whiskers. "What must I do to persuade you that I am innocent?"

My father smiled. "I have a proposal."

CHAPTER XVII

Ellie

I knew Claude and Edmund saw us being captured by Jonathan's men—the question was did they know how to rescue anyone from some guards?

The answer was probably yes, although they might not have been as skilled at it as Zach and I were. I tried not to keep glancing back to see what they were up to. I had to have faith that they would get out of this predicament—or at least help make a distraction so the three of us could knock these guards out.

I wasn't sure if Zach or Cor knew Claude and Edmund were following us. I had to believe that they did and that they wouldn't do anything to screw this up. I had to have faith in them.

It was hard to believe in anyone after everything we had been through. I had faith in Zach, of course, as he had been the only person I could trust for the past three years, but that was it. Everyone else had either been sent to kill us, wanted to kill us, or more often than not, both.

The guards weren't the worst we had dealt with, but they weren't exactly kind either. One of the guards had my arm in his hands, squeezing so I didn't run off. He had a tight grip.

It wasn't as if I could—they were armed, and we were shackled.

Cor stared off, as if disassociating with reality. I couldn't blame him—he had run away from the Kausians, fearing that they were going to kill him, and now he faced the same inevitable fate we all were facing constantly. The fate of death.

This was going to be our last chance to try to save this world, and we blew it. We had given up everything for this chance, and now I wasn't sure what would happen. Was Jonathan going to win over the Lyran governor? Would humans take over Mu?

I pushed those thoughts away. First things first—we had to get away from these guards and try to help Gabe. Perhaps we would be able to convince the governor as well, but I knew that would be pushing it. Would anyone believe some Kausians like us?

Trying not to draw attention to the two that would be saving us, I glanced back over to find Claude and Edmund still following us but from a distance. We were in the street, and if they did anything, they would draw attention. It wasn't like anyone was going to question some Kausians being arrested. They would think we were the bad guys.

No, they were going to wait until we were back to wherever Jonathan wanted us. It would be easier that way. Hopefully it wouldn't be too far. That would be the smart thing to do.

But they didn't know all this and of course attacked the guards in the open street with everyone watching.

Even I jumped, not expecting them to try anything. Claude and Edmund attacked the two guards that were behind Zach and Cor. With some loud thuds, they lay on the ground, unconscious.

Instead of letting go, the guard spun me in front of himself and placed the gun to my head.

"Freeze or she gets a bullet through her head!"

I had been yelled at by many guards, but the man's voice sounded familiar.

"Hey," I gasped out. "Did you work at the mansion we were just at?"

"Shut up!"

I had a feeling he had been there the night we ran away. And I had a feeling I might have shot him with some tranqs. That was why he didn't trust me. Couldn't blame him—many guards figured since I was a girl that I couldn't be a fighter—or they thought I was weak even if I could throw a few punches. Not many of them realized I had won quite a few shooting competitions over the years with all types of guns.

Claude and Edmund froze as did Cor and Zach. Although we outnumbered this guard, there wasn't much any of us could do with the gun against my skull.

And I had a feeling he would be pretty trigger happy if we threatened him.

I glanced around and saw some Lyrans running toward us. They were clearly guards, and they were clearly not going to believe some Kausians instead of Jonathan's guards.

"Go!" I exclaimed. "I will be fine! They will arrest you if you don't get out of here now."

The four of them ran before they could convince themselves to do something stupid. I would get out of this—I always did. All of them getting arrested wasn't going to help anyone.

"Do you really think you will be fine? I know what Jonathan has in store for you, and it's not pretty."

"I'll have you know I've been threatened at least five times a day since I started venturing outside of Kaus. Probably even before that. I am not afraid of you or Jonathan or anyone else."

He rammed his fist into my stomach. I knelt down, coughing. It had been a while since I had been punched in the stomach. It was strange—it almost felt nostalgic. That definitely wasn't normal.

The guard pulled me back up as the Lyran officers approached.

"Is there a problem here?" one of them asked.

"Those four that ran are enemies of the state.

Jonathan Pickett, standing leader of the humans, wants them arrested. Capture them and bring them to his estate."

The officers nodded and ran after Zach and the others. I knew Zach could escape them, as we had ran from Lyran officers many times, but I worried for the others.

"Come on!" The guard yanked me toward what I assumed would be Byron's old place—the place that started this entire mess.

As we approached, I found that I was right—we were, in fact, going to Byron's town house in the Human Zone. I laughed a little.

"Jonathan was quick to take over all of Byron's estates, wasn't he?"

"All the estates were co-owned. Their father made sure of that."

I let out a laugh. "To stop tension between the two? It's clear that didn't work."

The guard didn't say anything more as he shoved me inside. I glanced around, seeing if anything changed. It hadn't—everything was in the same spot that it had been when Byron brought us only a month before.

Which meant I knew how I was going to escape.

That is, if I could convince the guard to take me into the study. I had a feeling that was not where he was ordered to keep me.

As we walked inside, he started to push me down the hall. I tried to stop.

"Wait, can't we get a drink first? I know I'm parched from hiking as far as I did to get here."

The guard let out a huff. "You can't be serious—do you really think I am going to serve you alcohol?"

"Why not? Jonathan isn't here. Haven't you ever wanted to try something from his whiskey cabinet? I assume you guards never get to try the selection he has in his cabinet."

I noticed the guard's face twitch.

"No, you are trying to get me drunk so you can run off."

I shook my head. "It would take more than just a sip to get one with your build drunk enough to escape from. I just remember what I had last time I was here and want some more of it before, well, Jonathan kills me."

He hesitated. "There are other guards here—they will report me."

"Then send them out to fetch the two bodies of

the other guards. Someone needs to go clean up that mess before you start to gain attention. It wouldn't look good for whatever Jonathan has in store, now would it?"

With the distraction of having to bring me back here, he had completely forgotten about them—I could see it all over his face. He called out to the hallway.

"Reynolds, Smith! I have a task for you!"

I tried not to betray my eagerness as he ordered the two to go fetch the bodies down the street. It would take them at least a half an hour to go get the fallen guards and bring them back. That was plenty of time.

The two guards left us, and I smiled. "So what have you decided? Steal a drink or trap me in a room, bored out of my mind?"

The guard eyed me. "I won't say no to a drink."

"Great. Well, my hands are tied, so you lead the way."

He grabbed my arm, somewhat less tightly than earlier, and led me to the study. "Don't think I will be letting you out of those cuffs anytime soon. I am not that stupid."

"I wouldn't dream it."

He led us to the study and sat me down on the couch, careful not to turn his back to me. He's smart in that regard. I glanced at the mantel of the fireplace. As someone who had to often break out of houses such as this, I was able to get layouts of buildings and learn that there were quite a few different hideaways and escape routes for these rich folk. They never trusted anyone. I couldn't blame them—I didn't trust anyone either.

Hence why I knew about the routes.

I was pretty sure that was what that mantelpiece was—a handle that opened the back of the fireplace to be able to go into the sewers and get away in case one, I don't know, was wanted for genocide or something. The question was, how did I distract this guard long enough to make him not notice my escape?

I was probably going to have to knock him out, but this guy was on his guard—probably because I had knocked him out before. I guess I was going to have to resort to old tactics that I used when Zach and I were bounty hunters.

That meant I was going to have to seduce him.

I hated doing that—especially since I wasn't exactly dressed for seducing at the moment, but to be honest, that didn't matter. Men were men.

The guard poured the drinks and handed me a glass. He filled it a lot more than I thought he would, which would work to my advantage. I had a feeling I could hold my liquor better than he could.

"So." I twirled the drink around. "What do you think? Smooth, isn't it?"

He took a sip and tried not to cough. I laughed.

"Someone can't hold his liquor I see." I took a few sips of my own, not making a racket like he did.

"I just haven't had something this strong in quite a while, all right?"

I set the glass down and leaned forward. "What else haven't you done in quite a while?"

I saw his face flush, and it wasn't from the alcohol. He started coughing.

"Excuse me?"

With my bound hands, I traced his chest. "You know us Kausians can transform into whatever you like. Perhaps a blonde?" I changed my hair color. "Or perhaps you like redheads." I used my powers to change it again.

He shook his head, but he didn't move. "I'm not falling for this."

"Come on, those men will be gone for a good half an hour. We could have a little fun." I moved on top of his lap and whispered into his ear, "I mean, what else are we Kausians good for besides sex?"

The man tried to move, but he didn't put much effort into it. "I can't—if they find out."

"How would they find out? I can be whatever you want me to be." I transformed into a Sirian. "Perhaps this is more your style, hmm?"

That seemed to do it as he surrendered himself and grabbed my chin and began to kiss me. I guided him to move on top of me so I was on my back lengthwise on the couch.

And my hands were in reach of my whiskey glass.

I grabbed it and smacked him over the head with it. He went down like a sack of potatoes. I shoved him off me and rifled through his pockets for the keys to my cuffs. Just as I unlocked them, the fireplace back wall moved.

In a swift move, I grabbed the guard's gun and pointed it at the fireplace just as Zach stuck his head through the hideaway. I let out a sigh.

"Zach, I almost shot you."

He glanced at the guard on the ground. "How did you manage that?"

I rolled my eyes. "Never mind, let's go."

CHAPTER XVIII

Zach

Ellie totally used her feminine wiles to knock out
that guard. I had seen her use them before to get
out of situations and to capture a target, just like
she tried with Gabe. She wasn't going to admit it
though as she hated admitting she was attractive.
She also didn't like to show any sort of femininity,
which was fine. We all liked and disliked our own
thing. I just figured she could have gotten away
with a lot more if she actually played the part of the

damsel in distress. But that wouldn't make her the hard-ass she wanted to be.

Luckily Cor didn't see what I had seen or else he would have made a lot of comments—especially since we made fun of him anytime he used the same tactics to get what he wanted. Cor would have enjoyed seeing Ellie in some of the outfits she had used while we were bounty hunters to catch her mark. She would have been so embarrassed.

Cor, Claude, and Edmund were down in the sewer system waiting for us. I wasn't sure if there would be guards coming through this way so I decided it would be best if they stayed down here. If I ran into trouble, they could come get us out of it. I was taking a guess as to where the exit of this hideaway ended up, and I was glad I was right. That and I remembered Ellie telling me about it after we first met with Byron. I was happy that memory stayed in there. Usually directions didn't.

"Did you all have any trouble getting the Lyran officers off your tail?" Ellie asked as she transformed back into herself.

Yup, I was glad Cor didn't see that. Or Claude, for that matter.

"No trouble at all. You know how they are—easy

to distract them." I glanced at her to see if she would react to my comment. She didn't.

"Good. We are going to have to act fast—we need to go straight to the governor and tell him the truth," Ellie said.

I shook my head. "He's not going to believe us—not with Jonathan there. You realize all these aristocrats know each other, right? And they know that if they stand up to one of the others that they will all stab him in the back. He would be risking a lot if he tries to stand up to Jonathan."

"That is why we have to act now. It is our last chance. Besides, we know that Byron messed up what Jonathan was doing in the Sirian Zone. Perhaps Byron also messed up Jonathan's plan for the Lyran Zone, and Jonathan doesn't know that yet. He might act rash and use the wrong threat. Also, it's clear he is afraid of us and doesn't want us talking to the Lyran leader."

"What makes you say that?"

"He's going out of his way to cause us trouble. He fears us. He waited until we were here, knowing we could undo everything he's worked so hard to build. He has doubt about the Lyran governor, and we have to use that against him."

She had a point there. Why did he wait so long? Was he waiting to see what our next move would be? If so, what did that matter? We were just a couple of Kausians. Why was he so afraid of us?

"Maybe not everyone wanted to attack Kaus," Ellie went on. "Maybe the Lyrans stayed out of it, knowing perhaps it was wrong but didn't want to say anything for fear of what Byron and Jonathan might do."

"Which means he fears the Lyrans will side with what is right."

She nodded. "The Silurians wanted us gone, and Sirians have always wanted to stay out of any land affairs. Perhaps the Lyrans have noticed what is going on and are willing to set things straight once and for all."

We came to where I entered from the sewer, and Cor, Claude, and Edmund were all waiting for us. Claude's eyes practically sparkled when he saw Ellie. He grabbed her and twirled her in his arms.

"Thank the goddess you are fine! I was so worried!"

The look of shock was apparent on Ellie's face. "I… I'm fine. There is no need for this."

"Ellie's right," I commented. "We have been

arrested and captured countless times. If we celebrated every time, well, nothing would ever get done."

Claude set Ellie down. Although she was clearly wanting to head toward the capitol building and not fuss about, I could see her begin to blush. She was enjoying his worry for her.

Cor, though, was frowning. He didn't say anything, but I could tell he wanted to. Whether it was about Ellie getting away or how Claude was acting, I wasn't sure. If I had to guess, however, it was probably the latter, but had he known how Ellie had gotten away, he would have poked fun at her.

Ellie led the way out of the sewer. How she was able to memorize all the plans, both street and otherwise, of each town, I had no idea. She had always been fascinated by maps, however, and growing up, her room was filled with the things. She knew all of Mu like the back of her hand, which was why Cor always trusted her when they were making some ridiculous plan together. Perhaps that was why she was so good at memorizing maps—to keep Cor out of trouble.

"Did any of the Lyran officers see you go into the

sewer?" Ellie asked as she wound back and forth through the maze.

I was lucky I was able to even find Jonathan's estate. "No," I said. "I made sure no one saw us."

"It wasn't easy getting down here," Edmund added. "I'm surprised you would have even known how."

"There is a lot you don't know about me, big brother." Ellie sighed. "Three years can change someone."

Cor let out a laugh. "We were venturing through sewers long before that. Don't lie to him."

Ellie gave Cor a look. "But those adventures aren't anything he needs to know about."

"Thank you, Cor, for reminding me how much I hated you and how often you put my dear sister in trouble. I appreciate that."

"Don't mention it." Cor grinned.

I glanced at Ellie to find her trying to hold back a smile. Edmund really did hate Cor, and it started long before everything with Kaus and Byron. Cor would get into a lot of trouble and drag Ellie along with him. And me as well.

"Well, don't worry, Ellie. Once all this is over, I will keep you safe and out of all these messes,"

Claude said as he wrapped his arm around her waist.

I laughed. "Good luck with that. Ellie is just as bad as Cor when it comes to getting into trouble. We have been running into nothing but trouble for the past three years."

"Yeah? And whose fault is that?" Edmund added as he glared at Cor. "I mean, whose fault is it that we have no home to go to?"

Ellie glared at him. "This is not the time or place, Edmund. First, we have to stop an all-out war from happening. Then you can yell at Cor, okay?"

Edmund grunted but agreed. Cor didn't say anything but kept looking down, disassociating with what was going on around him.

I felt a little bad for Cor even though I knew he deserved it. Ellie could only stop so much at this point, mainly because it was her brother and the man she was dating, but if we did stop this war and the Kausians did decide to leave the mountains, where did he fit into the equation? It wasn't as if he could actually go back to living with them all. He couldn't exactly go home.

Although the Kausians would be mad that we broke Gabe out of jail, I doubted they would truly hold it against us—especially if we saved all of Mu. But Cor… even if he helped us, they were still going to blame him for everything, not to mention he was hunting Kausians to get more information about Krax. They weren't going to forgive him for that, and I didn't know if I really could. I was still mad at Ellie for hiding that information from me. When did she find out? How did she know?

Had he been hunting us? Was that why Ellie knew?

I didn't want to know the answer to that. Even if he had been, we had been hunting him, so it was only fair. We had pissed off a lot of people, so it would only make sense that he would have been given a contract to hunt us.

The question was, would he have gone through with it? Would he have killed the two of us just to get closer to Krax? I doubted it, but I didn't know how many of the Kausians he killed or handed over to people who would kill them were people we knew. Even if no one really cared about us and they saw us as problem children, I wouldn't have been able to betray any of them.

How could he have been so cold? How could he have been so desperate?

These were questions I wanted to ask him, but Ellie was right—they would have to wait. We had to focus on the task at hand.

Ellie approached a large metal door. "This is it—this will lead us to the capitol. Are we all ready?"

"What are we going to tell him?" Edmund asked.

"Simple," Ellie said as she began to rotate the wheel to open the door. "The truth."

CHAPTER XIX

Cor

I couldn't see this ending in any other way other than with our arrest, but I wasn't going to say that out loud—especially since I knew we were all thinking it. Ellie had one thing right—this was our last chance. If we didn't stop Jonathan now, this entire planet was doomed. Which was exactly what he wanted.

I didn't understand why anyone would want such a thing. What made this planet so fun was having a diverse population, and yet there was so much prejudice between the nations. Perhaps since my people received the most prejudice that I could actually see it. How amazing with this planet be if we got along and worked together? What could we accomplish?

Even if we won and stopped Jonathan, I doubted the nations would all get along—but one could dream. Perhaps it would at least be the start of something amazing.

Edmund helped Ellie rotate the wheel for the hatch. I was surprised it turned at all as a lot of these doors were locked or stuck from not having been used for so long. It made me a little worried, if I were honest—but I supposed that would have been something Byron or Jonathan would make sure was working in case either of them needed to escape. I watched as they pulled and cool, fresh air came pouring out of the entrance.

"Well then," Ellie said as she dusted herself off. "Shall we?"

My heart began to race. Why were we doing this again? Oh yeah—because we had to. I took a deep breath and followed behind Zach as we all entered what Ellie claimed to be the capitol. How Ellie was so good at memorizing maps and knew which door lead where was beyond me. It was clear she didn't lose that ability while on the run for three years. In fact, she probably had become more skilled at it. One needed to know the best ways to escape and hide—especially if they were Kausian.

Ellie led us up the stairwell. I wondered where this would end up. In the governor's office? In a bathroom? In the lobby? I hoped it was the former as then we wouldn't have to search for the governor and because I doubted anyone would let us see the governor—especially with how we looked and smelled.

I also wondered if Jonathan was still there and what sort of lies he would tell the governor. Would the governor believe him? Would he just take a look at us and claim that we were not worth listening to? If I were in his shoes, I wasn't sure if I would even believe us. We were just a group of Kausians who were known to cause mischief—even before the attack. No other country respected us.

And even if we stopped this war, would that even change? Would we even be accepted? I knew I wouldn't be accepted by anyone, but that was my own fault. The Kausians had every right to hate me. People in the other nations didn't know the truth, but they hated me because I was a Kausian. But would helping stop and all-out war make people accept us? Would we finally stop having to worry that we were going to be attacked? Would Ellie finally get a home she deserved away from the prejudice and constant fear for her life? That was all I had ever wanted for her, even back then. Which was exactly what Byron used to his advantage.

I pushed those thoughts away. I needed to focus. I needed to help convince the governor the truth— Jonathan was trying to rule this planet, and he wasn't going to stop until every other nation was destroyed. All the other stuff could wait. Besides, it still would take some time, and I knew that. There would be a lot of clean up for all the nations.

As we went through the passage, I found that we were in some kind of basement. It made sense since we had been in the sewer system—it wouldn't have dumped us onto the main floor of the building. I glanced around to find old documents, maps, plans for the city, and so on all scattered about. I saw Ellie hesitate as she saw them all, as if she wanted to investigate and learn more about the city's layout. I patted her on the back.

"Not now, all right? Maybe later you can deep dive into those maps."

She rolled her eyes. "I was just scanning to see where we were. I wasn't being tempted."

That was a total lie, and we both knew it. "Right."

She didn't say anything more and headed toward the stairs that would lead us up to the main floor. I felt my heartbeat quicken. I didn't want to do this —I didn't want to face Jonathan and the Lyran governor. After everything we had been through—after being betrayed by everyone we had asked for help from—I had no hope left. I didn't believe the Lyran governor would help us—I didn't believe we could actually stop Jonathan. I didn't even believe we could save our own skin. We were being hunted no matter where we went—me more than the rest.

I had thought we would be safe with the Kausians—but fear crept into my heart that they would find out the truth and want to execute me, and I had been right. Someone revealed what I had done, and they would have killed me if I hadn't run away. And I couldn't blame them—I deserved everything that was thrown at me.

This was all my fault.

No matter how many times Ellie tried to tell me that all this would have happened even if I didn't give the codes to Byron, I couldn't help but feel guilty. I should have stood my ground. I should have warned more people. I should have confessed what happened and helped wherever I could. Instead, I became a bounty hunter, and I delivered Kausians to the Silurians. I knew what would happen—I knew they would be killed. But I thought it would help me get closer to Krax, and I would finally make him pay.

And it wasn't even Krax that was responsible.

I felt like such a fool. But I had to do what I could to make it right or die trying. It was the only thing I could do at this point.

"If I'm not mistaken, the governor's offices should be three doors down to the left," Ellie said as she cracked open the door to the corridor. "Yeah, I'm certain that is the one."

"Wow, Ellie, you really do know your way around all the towns, don't you?" Claude asked.

She shrugged. "It's nothing, really. I just have good spatial awareness. That, and instead of learning all the other stuff in school, I decided to memorize directions and the maps of different cities. But also, a couple of Jonathan's guards are standing outside the door over there."

I peeked through the crack of the door. Sure enough, she was right—two of Jonathan's guards were standing there.

"Two guards won't be hard to take out," I commented. "We have done it before."

"Yes, but," Ellie said as she slowly closed the door again, "the problem is that we have to take them out without anyone noticing. Otherwise, we'll be dealing with many more guards, and I don't particularly want to fight a bunch of Lyrans when we're trying to get on their good side."

She had a point.

Edmund said, "It will be hard not to stand out in these clothes. We smell disgusting and are covered in filth."

He was right—we couldn't just transform into Lyrans and hope for the best. I feared they would be able to smell us even from the other side of this door.

I watched as Ellie glanced around. "If this basement is, in fact, for storage, maybe there are some spare uniforms. Let's split up and see if we can find anything."

Nodding, we all went in different directions and began to glance at the labels on all the boxes. Most of them were categorized, so it was easy to check, but there were also some that were either too old and worn to read the label or simply didn't have one. I began ripping open ones that didn't have tags.

I found extra paper, staples, ink, other office supplies, but I had no luck finding any sort of uniform. I was beginning to think we wouldn't find anything when I heard Claude shout.

"Found something!"

Of course it had to be him that found something. I let out a breath as I hurried over with the others to see what he'd found. Sure enough, it was a crate full of uniforms.

Ellie gave him a kiss on the cheek. "Good job, Claude."

She glanced to me, and I quickly turned away. While I knew Ellie should find happiness somewhere else, that didn't mean I wanted to see it.

"Okay, everyone find your sizes. If we are convincing enough, we should be able to walk into

brother did most of the heavy lifting, but now it was all him. Because he had killed his own brother. And his own wife.

And he tried to kill me, and I was pretty sure after today was over, he was going to finish the job. Or maybe he would wait and find some other use for me and kill me once I was no longer valuable to him.

Part of me was glad my mother wasn't here to see what sort of monster he really was.

If I said anything to this Lyran, who knew damn well that the footage was fake, my father would kill the only people I ever considered to be friends—that is, if Claude and Edmund hadn't saved them yet. Although I hoped for the best, for all I knew, the two of them could have been caught, and Jonathan could have them all. So I would keep playing along, and pray to the goddess that they were fine.

"You want me to hand over my power to you is what you are saying?" Riazusryz asked.

That was what my father was asking—he wanted to be one of the council members, along with other people in his circle. The council were the ones who made a lot of decisions for the Lyran Zone. They could do whatever they wanted, including starting a war.

And, of course, he would get them to start a war with the Sirians and increase their efforts against the Silurians.

Although the Silurian's had the most advanced technology, Lyran had the most manpower and were some of the fiercest warriors on the planet. And the people wouldn't question a war—not when a lot of them loved fighting. In fact, elected officials had to do whatever they could to keep them from starting a war.

So, perhaps, that was why Riazusryz believed the footage to be real—he knew some of his people wanted war and they might set him up for it. Then he would have to declare war.

Jonathan smiled. "That is exactly what I am asking."

Riazusryz shook his head. "I can't allow that. Only Lyrans can be on the council—you know that is our custom. The people would riot."

My father shrugged. "You can easily appoint whoever you want. The people love me, and after they see what happened to my brother, they will come to agree with me being on the council. I don't think you will have any sort of uprising."

Riazusryz brought his hands together. "I think you think way too highly of yourself, Jonathan. You are not your brother."

I could feel my father's anger rise. It was as if an electric wave went through the room even though I knew it hadn't. I was so used to people's moods changing drastically when I was growing up—mainly due to Byron—that I was always hyperaware of what people's emotions were.

I wasn't sure if Riazusryz could tell how angry he was, as Jonathan hid it behind a smile, but it was there. I could sense it. Though I had a feeling, due to the Lyran's keen sense of smell.

"I take offense to that, Riazusryz. While my late brother was definitely the socialite, many of his friends preferred my presence rather than his."

Riazusryz let out a laugh. "They were trying to be nice, Jonathan. Many of them found you to be insufferable. Your brother made sure of that. He didn't trust you and for good reason. I have reason to believe that footage you have is fake, and it was, in fact, you that killed your own brother due to your jealousy."

I felt my lip twitch, wanting to turn into a smile,

but I knew my father wouldn't have that. So Riazusryz wasn't convinced—he was just playing the part to learn what my father wanted to do. I had to hand it to him, he was clever.

Jonathan frowned. He wasn't masking his anger any longer. "How dare you accuse me of fratricide! My brother and I might have had our differences, but it wasn't enough for me to kill him!"

Riazusryz stood up and peered out the window. "You are the one that came in here claiming someone killed your brother from the Lyran Zone. Even if it were true, that doesn't mean I had anything to do with it. If you really want to keep threatening me, I can have that video analyzed by tech experts to see if it has been tampered with or not.

"Meanwhile, I suggest you take your family drama somewhere else. I know it was you and your brother behind the attack on the Kaus Zone, and I don't know how, but Byron was behind the ordeal that was on Xynon just a few weeks ago. And don't think I don't know about your son wanted for matricide. Your family is full of drama, Jonathan, and I don't want any part of it."

Jonathan's mouth dropped. I was also surprised

that Riazusryz would speak so frankly—especially when he knew it was my father behind all those things. Didn't he know if he refused, my father would escalate the matter? That we would find some other way to gain power?

Before my father could respond, the door to the office opened.

"Sir, these three said that they had an urgent matter and needed to speak to the governor."

The two guards my father appointed in the corridor stepped inside the office, followed by three faces I didn't expect to see until all this was over.

Ellie, Zach, and Cor rushed inside and quickly shut the door behind them. With their stun guns, they shot Jonathan's guards.

Turning to Riazusryz, Ellie quickly said, "Sir, I can explain! The man killed his brother in cold blood and is manipulating—"

Riazusryz held up his hand. "I already had my suspicion—you need not to continue, ma'am. This man here was just leaving."

I couldn't believe what I was hearing—was someone going to finally take our side in this battle? Would Riazusryz help us take Jonathan out, or was he just going to stay neutral? Before any of us could ask, my father grabbed me and pulled me in front of him. I felt a gun jam into my side.

"Before the three of you get any bright ideas, I will be taking my son with me. I miss him oh so much, and we need some quality time together."

"You tried to kill him last time you saw him," Cor exclaimed. "Let him go!"

Jonathan shook his head. "No. Now back away, or I will shoot him. And this time, I won't mess up."

I watched the three of them hesitate, but then they backed away. I was doomed to be my father's hostage. If it weren't for me, they could have killed Jonathan here and now. But I was in the way.

Why was I such a liability?

"If you hurt him, I will hunt you down and murder you myself," Cor growled.

"Well then, you better not follow me. If I see any of you, I will immediately kill him. You got that?"

They didn't move, knowing he wasn't bluffing. My father would kill me—I meant nothing to him. I was just a means to an end. He sired me just to further his plot.

I wanted to tell them to go ahead and stop him now—let me die as it was my fate—but my voice was caught in my throat. Perhaps I didn't want to die—perhaps I wanted my father to face justice. Perhaps I wanted to end his life myself.

Before I could say anything—before the others could make their move—my father dragged me out of the office and went straight to his carriage where the rest of his guards were waiting.

"Go! Now!" he commanded them as he threw me in the carriage. I hit the opposite side with a thud as he shut the door behind him.

My father pointed down at me. "You! This is your fault! You didn't make it convincing!" He kicked me in the stomach.

"I'd rather die than for your plan to succeed. Do what you will—they will stop you. All your work will be for nothing!"

Father kicked me again. I groaned on the ground of the carriage as it began to move.

"No, this part of the plan wasn't necessary. I can bring down the Lyran Zone just like I did the others. And I will make you watch as I destroy everything you have ever loved."

Getting up, I watched as the capitol building disappeared in the distance. I just hoped the others would be able to get Riazusryz to side with them.

CHAPTER XXI

Ellie

How was it that Jonathan always seemed to have the upper hand? He still had Gabe, and I had no idea if he was going to kill him right away or if he was going to hold on to him to use him against us later.

It would probably be the latter, but I couldn't say for certain. We needed to help him, but first things first though.

I turned to Riazusryz. "Governor Riazusryz,

please listen to us before you call your guards."

He's gestured around. "If I wanted my guards here, I would have already called them. I know you all are Kausians—I can tell by your eyes. And I have a feeling I know why you are here."

I glanced at Cor and Zach. They seemed just as puzzled.

"You do?" I asked.

He nodded as he took a seat. He gestured at the other chairs in the room. "Please sit down. Now tell me why I should side with you and not Jonathan, not that I trust a thing anyone from that family says."

So there was some hope left in the world. The three of us took a seat. Claude and Edmund decided to stay in the basement for two reasons: as back up and to keep out of Jonathan's radar. We didn't know when we might need an element of surprise to gain the upper hand again. While his men might have told him there were other Kausians out there helping us, unless he got close enough to see their eyes, he didn't know what they looked like. Not yet, anyway.

"Now start from the beginning. How are you three involved in this mess? Besides being

Kausians, of course."

I glanced at Cor. He hesitated, but he started the story. "Our home was destroyed three years ago because of me. I fell for Byron's lies and thought he would give me an actual education—I thought he would help me get into a Human University, but it was all a setup. He just wanted me to give him the codes of the shield that protected Kaus from invaders."

He nodded. "I knew Byron got that info some sleazy way, but I never imagined it was by using the kid that he used to mentor. I remember seeing you with him in passing. I was as fooled as you and thought he was actually helping you. I should have known better—I knew he and his family were up to something."

"If you don't mind me asking," I said. "How did you know the family was manipulating people?"

Riazusryz sighed as he tapped his desk. "Byron would sometimes drink more than he could handle, and he would say some of the most obscure things, like how his grandfather was a smart man and wanted to take over the world or how the Kausians used to be a great nation until his grandfather stopped that. Then I looked into it. I found some of the old history books that his family took out of schools—and sure enough, there were records of how advanced the Kausians used to be."

I couldn't believe what I was hearing. Jonathan's family had rewritten history. Even us Kausians had no idea. Sure, some of the elders used to say how advanced we were, but none of us actually believed them—how could we? We could barely get by—all we need was the shield, which was advanced, I supposed.

Had all our technology been like that? Could we restore it all?

"I looked more into what books were used in schools, what companies donated what, and I found such a web of deceit that I didn't even know what to believe anymore. Byron and Jonathan's family have had their grubby fingers in so many things for so long—I knew there was something they were after. So, over the past decade or so, I have been slowly plucking some of the things that the two of them own and slowly Jonathan and Byron have been losing their power without either of them noticing. They are so caught up in destroying other nations they haven't even noticed their own power has been dwindling. I, of course, made sure those companies kept face with them, until the time comes, and we turn on them. Which, I suppose, will be sooner rather than later now."

That was a lot to take in. Riazusryz had known this entire time about Byron and Jonathan. He was on our side—or, at least, he wasn't on Jonathan's side. He didn't want to be a part. Of their madness. He was going to listen to us.

"Then why didn't you stop him from destroying Kaus," Cor asked. "Why didn't you stop that from happening?"

Riazusryz shook his head. "I never imagined he would destroy it like he did. He must really fear you if he went after you all first. I mean, although your nation was one of the most advanced back in the day, you all weren't a threat by the time he came around. He really feared you. He probably feared you would learn the truth and regain that technology."

"it probably wasn't our technology as much as it is the fact we can change our appearance," Cor said. "He probably thought we could somehow use it against him, when really we can't. Or, at least, not that easily. Our eyes give us away. Everyone knows that."

"Perhaps, but perhaps not. I think he was afraid of how diligent and strong-willed your kind can be."

I didn't know if one could say that about all Kausians, as most Kausians were in hiding, not to mention they didn't want anything to do with another zone even when we were all still in Kaus. I doubted they would have stood up to Byron if he attacked any other zone first. So we couldn't exactly blame Riazusryz for not stopping Byron from destroying Kaus—especially when it could jeopardize his own people.

"Now," he said. "Tell me, how did you three get wrapped up in this? Besides with what happened three years ago."

I answered, "We happened to get caught up with what happened on Xynon." I glanced at Zach. "Long story short, he used our power to make the Silurian forces attack the people there. After that, we escaped to the Sirian Zone, hoping Gabe's mother would side with us and stop Byron."

"But that backfired," Zach commented. "Because Byron knew that was where we would go, and he used a different Kausian to transform into Gabe and had him kill his mother."

"She was going to help us too," I said. "But instead, we made everything worse. We escaped, but the moment we got to shore, we were arrested for some other crime Byron pinned on us. We all broke out of prison except for Cor here. Byron took him to their home where Jonathan was. While we were trying to break Cor out of the mansion, Gabe tried to win his father over to help stop Byron, but he could never have imagined that his father was the one really behind this. He tried to poison Gabe, and, well, we barely escaped with our lives."

I stopped there, knowing we couldn't exactly tell him about the Kausians. They would have our heads if that were the case, not that they didn't already.

"Then we came here," Zach lied. "Knowing it was our last chance in getting some sort of help in taking Jonathan down. He is going to try to destroy all nonhumans on Mu. We can't let that happen."

Riazusryz took a moment to take in everything we said. It was a lot—I had to agree. And it all happened within a month.

"Well." He let out a sigh. "You three have had quite the adventure, haven't you?"

"You could say that," I commented.

"I will bring this information to the council. If I have my way, we will declare war on Jonathan. We have been in talks for a couple of weeks now, knowing he has been up to something. This will be enough for our people to declare war."

My heartbeat quickened. Was I hearing right? Was he going to help us?

After all this time, we finally found the help we needed. Not only was someone listening to us, but he had the power of an entire nation to back us up. He believed in Kausians and respected them—I didn't even know that was possible.

What did that mean for us after this war? Did that mean we could send word to the Kausians and we could rebuild our city? Did that mean there were records we could find of our old nation and the technology we once had? Would children finally get proper schooling and be accepted no matter where they went?

I was getting ahead of myself, I knew. But it was the first time in a long time I actually had hope.

Riazusryz went on. "For now how about you all get cleaned up? I will have some rooms prepared for you all. I will alert my secretary to take you to the hotel."

I responded. "That would be amazing, thank you! There are actually two more people outside; if you have four rooms, that would be enough."

He nodded. "Consider it done. I will call upon the council immediately and summon you later this evening. Until then, keep your eyes out for anything suspicious. Jonathan has people everywhere."

That we knew. We gave our thanks and headed toward the front desk. This all went smoothly, which made me worry. Nothing ever went smoothly.

CHAPTER XXII

Zach

Not only were we given rooms, but we were also given comfy beds. I wanted more than anything to jump on the mattress, but I didn't want to make it smell like a sewer, even with the new clothes we had stolen in the basement. Riazusryz's secretary said she would send us some clothes as well and dispose of our soiled ones. I took off my clothes, set them outside for whoever was coming around, and jumped in the shower.

The water was warm. I could probably even make it scalding hot, but I didn't want to cause an injury. Everything about this establishment was nice—it must have been where Riazusryz put up traveling dignitaries and what not. The lobby even had a large buffet with food that didn't appear to be spoiled. I would have to visit that buffet later as I was starving, and it had been a couple of days since I had a good meal. The thought of those pancakes I saw made my stomach growl.

After taking my time cleaning off to the point where I could no longer smell sewer, I stepped out of the shower to find a new outfit set out on the bed. Ellie and I usually had to bathe in cold water and had grown used to it, but when we could splurge on a warm bath, we did. There was nothing better than a hot bath. I quickly put the clothes on and found they were a size too big, but that was better than the opposite. There was a belt on the bed as well, and I used that to keep my pants up. Once I hit the buffet downstairs, perhaps these pants would fit perfectly.

Deciding to see if Ellie was also cleaned up, and if she wanted to grab a bite to eat, I left my room and made my way to the next room over. Riazusryz was able to get us four rooms all together, meaning all four of us were in the same hallway. Since there were four rooms and five of us, Ellie and Claude were sharing a room. I was surprised she requested such an arrangement, but the two of them were getting closer.

I knocked on their door, and Ellie answered. Her hair was wet, and she had already changed into some new clothes—a green dress with a white bow in front. I grinned at the frown on her face.

"What are you smiling about?" She spat.

"Heh. Nothing. Did Riazusryz make an assumption that since you were a girl you would wear a dress?"

She folded her arms in front of herself. "Just because I am a woman doesn't mean I like wearing a dress. They are such a hassle to deal with, not to mention I can't even run safely in this thing without tripping. Also, where do I put my gun?"

"Well, you look cute either way." I grinned.

She rolled her eyes. "Whatever, come on in. Claude is still in the shower, but Edmund and Cor should be showing up any moment now."

I stepped inside as Ellie kept fiddling with her dress. She really did hate dresses and only wore them when necessary. Riazusryz must have assumed she was wearing the uniform because it was the only thing she could find. I wondered if she would complain or if she would just deal with it since he was willing to pay for all of this.

I sat down on her bed, and soon after, there was a knock on the door. I answered it, as Ellie didn't want to move around any more than she needed to in her dress. It was both Cor and Edmund. Although they were standing next to one another, it was clear that they didn't want anything to do with each other. I couldn't blame either of them. Once this was all over, I had a feeling they would be happy if they never saw one another again.

They stepped inside, and I watched as Cor grinned at Ellie. "Well, well, someone looks nice."

She flipped Cor off as Claude stepped out of the bathroom. He was just in his towel. Edmund whistled at him as Claude's cheeks grew red. I quickly looked away, holding back my laughter.

"Oh," he said as he quickly grabbed his clothes. "I didn't realize the meeting would start so soon."

"Sorry." Ellie seemed genuine with her words. "I thought you took your clothes in there."

"No worries—I'll be right back."

I glanced at Cor, who seemed to be ignoring the whole situation. I couldn't imagine what it was like seeing your ex-fiancé dating another man—although Ellie had to witness him and Gabe this entire time, so I didn't really feel sorry for him.

Once Claude put some clothes on and came out of the bathroom, we began our meeting.

Ellie started, "Riazusryz said he would tell us the decision tonight on whether the council will go to war with Jonathan. By the sounds of it, they have been wanting to go to war with him for a while now—they have just needed a real excuse, and the information we gave them and Jonathan blackmailing them seems like it will be enough for them to officially declare war.

"The question is, how much backing does Jonathan really have? The nations have been attacking the Silurians—I think if the Lyrans moved their effort to the Human Zone, Jonathan's forces will be stretched a little too thin, not to mention Riazusryz said he has been stealing Jonathan's companies out from under him."

"If that is the case," Cor began, "it could also backfire and the Silurians could see that the Lyrans aren't attacking them any longer and might try to gain the upper hand and attack the Lyran Zone."

"That is something Riazusryz will have to decide although I highly doubt it. With the information we gave him, it might also be possible that he will contact whoever is now in charge of the Silurian Zone and see if they will put all their efforts against Jonathan," Ellie said. "We will make sure that is brought to his attention."

"Even with the two zones attacking the Human Zone," I started, "the Human Zone is large and strong. Jonathan's family has been planting xenophobic ideals in their people for generations. They have a lot of manpower and weapons. The Lyrans and Silurians will be outnumbered—or at least those who will be fighting. By the sounds of it, the Silurians have lost a lot of men already, and while the Lyran forces are strong, I'm not confident they will succeed in this."

Ellie nodded. "I'm worried about this too. We know the Sirians won't side with the Lyrans and will do whatever they can to stay out of this war." She turned to Edmund and Claude. "So we need more manpower."

Edmund shook his head. "Even if the Kausians wanted to fight, which they don't, there aren't many of us to make a difference in this war, Ellie.”

“I know you are right," Ellie said. "But, if this all goes downhill, I want you two to make a break for it and go back, all right? This isn't your war—you shouldn't deal with our mistakes."

Claude grabbed her hand. "No, we aren't running. We are here to see the end of this—just as you are."

"Besides," Edmund added. "We rather go back with good news of how the war is over, and it is safe to rebuild."

I nodded. "And we will. At least, I hope we will."

“And what about Gabe?” Cor asked. “How are we going to rescue him?”

Ellie took a long breath and let it out slowly. “I don’t know. We don’t know where Jonathan took him or if we would even be able to rescue him. We are so close to defeating his forces—if we turn our attention away from stopping him, we might lose everything.”

Cor narrowed his eyes. “So you are going to leave him?”

That’s what it sounded like to me. I glanced at Ellie, who was frowning. “We don’t know if he is alive, Cor. Last time Jonathan was with Gabe, he tried to murder him. He might kill him to get the

Sirians to side with him. He is desperate right now; you saw his face. He couldn't believe that Riazusryz didn't fall for his trick."

Clutching his hands into fists, Cor glared at Ellie. "We can't just assume he is dead. We have to do something—"

"Like what, Cor? Risk all this—risk stopping Jonathan once and for all—for someone who might be dead already?"

"Stop saying that! He wouldn't leave you behind, why are you leaving him behind?"

"No, but you left us behind. Many times. So are you going to leave again? Are you going to run off when we need you most? When I need you most?"

Cor and Ellie held each other's gaze for a moment, and then Cor got up and left the room.

CHAPTER XXIII

Cor

I slammed the door behind me. I couldn't believe what I was hearing—they were just going to leave him? How could they do that? After everything?

I took a deep breath and let it out slowly. Perhaps I wasn't really mad at them—perhaps I was just mad at myself for leaving him in the mountains. I was the one who left him behind—I left them all behind.

And I had no idea if he was alive. Ellie was right.

Jonathan could easily kill Gabe to try to win the Sirian support. He could tell them that he was siding with the Lyrans, which wasn't exactly false, but he would add lies about him killing the queen for the Lyrans and wanting to start a war. Then Jonathan would ask them to side with him and they would be able to suppress the Lyrans and the Silurians. Or perhaps he would keep him alive and use him as leverage against the Sirians.

Which meant I had to act fast and hope for the best. I had to go out there and see if I could find him. I couldn't betray him—not again.

But Ellie had a point—I would be leaving her behind again, and she would have to pick figure this all out without me. But she didn't need me. She had Claude. And her brother. And Zach.

She had moved on, and I couldn't blame her. I wasn't reliable. I had done horrible, unforgivable things. She finally found someone who would take care of her. If it weren't for me, she would still be with the Kausians. She would still have a home. But now she found herself in the middle of this war because I messed up. She deserved better.

Before I could decide on anything, there was a knock on the door. I opened it to find Ellie standing there, still in that cute dress the Lyrans had picked out for her. It didn't suit her at all, but she sure did look cute in it.

"Can I talk to you for a second?" Ellie asked, her voice softer than normal. I nodded and she stepped in.

"Look, I'm sorry if I sounded harsh earlier," she began.

I shook my head. "No, you weren't being harsh. You were being realistic. This is all my fault—none of you should be dealing with this. Gabe is my responsibility, and not only did I leave him behind with you on Kaus, I was always leaving him behind. He deserves better. You deserve better. All of this is because of me—I was the reason Byron gained so much control and took out our nation. None of you should be dealing with this."

Ellie shook her head. "I think even if you didn't give them the codes, Byron or Jonathan would have figured out some way to attack us. So you aren't completely to blame. In fact, we made it out alive because of you. Had they attacked some other way, perhaps we wouldn't have been so lucky."

I knew she was trying to make me feel better, but I couldn't help but still feel responsible. When it came down to it, I was the one who had given the codes. To all the others, I was responsible.

Not to mention all the people who died after the attack. No matter what anyone said, those were on my hands.

"I just… I can't leave him behind. Not after everything," I said.

Ellie nodded. "I know. You should go find him. Or, at least try."

I glanced at her, then looked back down at the ground. "I'm sorry I'm leaving you behind again."

"It doesn't matter anymore. I've moved on. I am capable of standing on my own two feet, Cor. If there was one thing you should be happy about, it's that you taught me to rely on myself."

I smiled a little. I knew she was joking, but it was true—she was strong because she had to deal with someone like me. I should be happy she was with Claude—I should be happy she found her own path, but it hurt. It hurt more than I ever could have realized.

There was silence again. How could I feel so awkward around someone I used to love so much?

"For what it's worth, I hope you are able to save him." With that, she left me in my room.

Deciding it was as good a time as any, I grabbed the bag with some extra supplies Riazusryz provided for us, along with some extra cash, and headed out the door.

I didn't know exactly where I should start looking. Jonathan and Byron's family had an estate in the Lyran Zone, but I had doubted he went back there. There might be clues, however, as to where they went. Deciding that was my best course of action, I headed toward the estate.

The estate brought back memories of Byron tutoring me. This was the place we would meet. His staff would serve us tea as he taught me about math, finance, history, grammar, and so on. All of it had simply been to gain my trust—none of it was actually from the goodness of his heart. I had been such a fool. Why did I think anyone would want to help a Kausian, let alone me?

I tried to push the memories back as I came upon the estate. It was evening now, but all the lights inside were off. Just as I expected, he'd left town in a hurry with whatever guards were stationed in there.

Grabbing one of the knives from my belt, I

worked on picking the lock. I had become an expert over the years as sometimes I would have to break into a building for my bounty hunter work. The opposite was needed for when I was sleeping around for money—then I would need to sneak out of a building rather than into one.

As I stepped inside, I noticed that the place had been ransacked. I shook my head. No, I was wrong. It hadn't been ransacked but packed up in a hurry. Jonathan had grabbed everything he needed or everything that could incriminate him and left this place behind.

Which meant there was probably no one here.

I would stay on high alert, however—one couldn't be too careful.

Keeping an ear out for any sound, I walked carefully through the entry toward the parlor where I used to meet with Byron. Memories called to me like ghosts. I could practically hear Byron beckoning me to sit down and listen to him lecture about whatever topic tickled his fancy that week. I blinked, and where I swear I saw him standing was nothing but darkness and overturned chairs.

He wasn't there. He was dead and now I had to stop his kin from destroying this land.

I took a deep breath and let it out slowly. It was all in my mind. I needed to focus.

There were papers scattered all around the room. I quickly skimmed them, looking for any signs as to where Jonathan could have moved to. Odds were, he would go back to his manor in the Human Zone, but I didn't want to travel all the way there to find that he wasn't there—especially with how highly guarded it was.

No, I had to find out for a fact where he was if I wanted to save Gabe.

As I flipped through more papers, I heard a noise from the other room. I pulled out my knife and slowly peeked out into the corridor. There was a faint light coming from the kitchen. I slowly crept forward, careful not to make a noise or trip over the random objects that had been scattered around.

I peeked into the kitchen to find a guard had, in fact, been left behind. He was wearing the same uniform as the other guards that Jonathan had around him earlier. It appeared that he was looking for a snack.

I pushed the door open and rushed at him with my knife before he could notice I was there. He stumbled backward, and I pinned him down with my legs and held the knife under his throat.

"If you want to live, tell me where Jonathan went!"

The man was still trying to process everything that had happened as his eyes darted all around.

"I... I... Don't—"

"Liar! He would have said while he was packing up! Tell me now, or you will die here and now," I growled.

Tears filled his eyes. "Please don't! I have a daughter and wife at home!"

"Then speak!"

The guard hesitated for a moment, and then he finally answered, "The port city of Tattingborough."

That was one of the closest port towns that could go down to the Sirian Zone. This was bad—this was exactly what we expected he would do.

Now the question was what did I do with this man? If I let him go, he would call ahead and warn Jonathan. Then Jonathan would go ahead with his plan, which more than likely included killing Gabe.

But this man was unarmed and was crying. I didn't want to be the man I used to be anymore—I didn't want any more blood on my hands.

However, if I didn't spill blood now, the one I loved might die.

Without any more hesitation, I sliced his throat. His eyes widened as he tried to breathe, but all that happened was blood came pouring out of the cut along his throat. I stood up before any more blood could spill on my clothes.

The man slowly died at my feet, and I watched as he stopped trying to gasp for air and finally lay still.

"I'm sorry."

CHAPTER XXIV

Gabe

I was sure I was going to die.

We were headed toward Tattingborough, one of the port cities in the Human Zone that led down to the Sirian Zone. I was sure my father would murder me and bring my severed head, or whatever, to whoever was now reigning in place of my sister. My sister would never know the truth of what happened, as Jonathan and others would spin so many lies that she would forget what she witnessed. She wouldn't remember it was me that held her as we watched our mother be killed. It would all seem like some kind of dream. She would think her brother was a murderer and come to hate me.

And that hurt more than any bullet or knife could.

I loved my sister very much. While she was little when I ran away from home, she was the purest thing I could ever love. My mother had me swear I protect her for as long as I lived, and I lived by that promise. She was the only one who listened to me, and she always looked up at me with such enduring eyes. I couldn't let this man manipulate her—I wouldn't let him. If I had to fight for anything, it would be for her.

I sat in the carriage, staring out the window, trying to come up with a plan, or ignore where I was at the moment—my brain hadn't quite decided which to do yet. My father was sitting across from me, and I didn't want to look at him. I didn't want to see the similarities we had—I didn't want to be reminded of the photos of when I was a baby and he stood there with my mother in his embrace. She had loved him with all her heart, but she was just a means to an end for him. It broke my heart. We had just been pawns in some kind of messed-up game.

A game that called for both my mother and my deaths.

Once we got to the port city, I would do what I could to try to escape, but with how many guards and people on Jonathan's side, it seemed inevitable I would die. No, I couldn't think that way—I had to find a way out of this.

"Don't look so depressed, my dear son. I am not going to kill you."

Even though I didn't want to look at him, I turned my head to face him in surprise—half because I had expected him to kill me, half wondering how he knew what I was thinking.

"I still need you for all this, but don't worry. I will, in fact, be using you to get the Sirians to side with us. But I need you alive if I am going to keep your dear friends in check. And besides, you are my son, and I want you to witness your family's legacy come to fruition."

I knew if I threw up right then and there, my father might go back on his word and kill me. I didn't respond to him, knowing he was trying to get a rouse out of me.

"It is not my legacy. I want no part in it," I said, my voice a little darker than I wanted.

He laughed. "Oh, but it is. And it was your grandfathers, and his father before him. So many decades of work, and it is all finally coming to an end. I am so glad my own son will get to see all my work pay off."

I had no words for him. I wanted to say the only thing I wanted to see come to fruition was his death. Was it wrong for me to want my own father dead? He had brought so much destruction to the world, including my own mother's death, and he had killed his own brother. He also tried to kill me —so no, I didn't feel bad for wanting such things. But when push came to shove, would I be able to end him?

The answer was probably not, but I knew I shouldn't be thinking like that. I shouldn't be weak when it came to him. I had to do it—I could possibly be the only one. Because he thought I was too weak and would never suspect me.

"First things first, though. We are going to the Sirian Zone. Won't it be nice to see your sister? Perhaps she can help with our efforts."

I glared at him. "She is just a child."

He smiled. "Exactly, and she needs some guidance. Perhaps I don't hand you over to the Sirians but tell them what really happened. Perhaps I tell them how Byron used them and that you avenged your mother by killing him. They will be at a loss because they for some reason helped Byron up to godlike status. Then you will be like a savior to them and can finally claim your right to the throne."

I had to admit, other than the fact that he was coming up with the plan, it didn't sound half bad. My sister would know the truth, and the idea of my people liking me sounded appealing. But I didn't believe it for a moment. "And then what? Do whatever you say? I will never help you."

He shrugged. "You either help me, or I will force your sister to help me. The choice is yours."

I hated this—I hated this manipulation. I had always looked up to him, and now I was coming face-to-face with his true nature.

"You disgust me."

Jonathan laughed. "My dear son, you need to learn that the only way to exist in this world is by being ruthless and not letting anyone get in your way."

I shook my head. "No—I'd rather live in a way that supports others. I'd rather have a community where I feel welcomed, and we all support each other."

He shook his head. "No such community exists."

I was about to open my mouth and say that he was wrong, but then he would ask questions, and I couldn't betray the Kausians like that—even if they were going to kill me. They had their reasons, especially after everything. If I ruined that for them, there would be no coming back. He would destroy what remaining Kausinas were left, and that would be that. And it would be all my fault. I wouldn't let that happen.

But perhaps he was right. Other than the Kausians in the mountains, there was no real community that got along so well. There were always people that would betray others—there were always people that would try to gain power—there was always corruption. I had seen it everywhere we had gone, but at the root of much of the corruption, both Jonathan and Byron were there. The Lyran saw that, so it had to be true.

But that didn't excuse what other people had done. It didn't excuse the Silurians for attacking the

Kausian city, and it didn't excuse the racism that I witness against the Kausians. Even with all the propaganda, it was still an individual's choice to view a person a certain way. The truth was out there—they just had to be willing to find it and not listen to so much hate and bigotry.

"What about Riazusryz? He seems to not fall for your corruption. He is standing up for justice, much to your surprise."

My father's face went dark. "He is not standing up for justice—he is being stubborn and not seeing how things need to be!"

I held my tongue, knowing my father might smack me if I said anything more. He was delusional if he seriously thought that. Riazusryz had bested him, and he didn't want to admit it.

Jonathan coughed and regained his composure. "At any rate, he will be taken down, and Lyran Zone will be under the rule of the humans, just as the Silurians will soon be. Then you will take the Sirian throne and do what I say if you want your sister to live a long and happy life. Do you understand me?"

I glared at him. I would figure a way out of this, but for now I had to play along. "Yes, Father."

He smiled. "Good. Now we are on the same page. I am glad you are starting to see reason."

I clenched my fists at my side. I wanted more than anything to punch him in his grinning face. But did I have that in me? Could I stop my father when it came down to it? Could I actually end his life, or would I have to let someone else dirty their hands?

CHAPTER XXV

Ellie

Riazusryz called us to his office about four hours after Cor left. The four of us were downstairs having a bite to eat. There was a huge spread of food in the lobby, and plenty of tables and chairs. I was surprised it wasn't more crowded with how much food there was—food that wasn't spoiled and had the right equipment to keep it warm or fresh.

Zach his fill, and then some. I noticed Edmund and Claude weren't stuffing their faces—I wondered if they felt guilty since the Kausians in the mountains didn't get to eat this much every day, but it would be a lie if I said the food there wasn't fantastic. It reminded me of home, especially since it essentially was. How they were able to still cook amazing meals was beyond me. It reminded me when we used to have the potlucks in town, and Cor would do something to get us kicked out—much to his parents' dismay.

It would be a lie if I said my heart didn't feel crushed that Cor chose going after Gabe instead of staying here with me. I knew it was selfish—I knew I shouldn't care what he chose anymore because I had Claude, but it still hurt.

But if Gabe was still alive, then he should go save him.

Claude held my hand as we walked over to the governor's office. He didn't say anything about Cor, but I could tell he was trying to comfort me. When we were younger, he had always tried to cheer me up when I was feeling down, which was usually because of Cor or something at school, if I did go to school. I wasn't the best student and got called to the teacher's office more often than not. I just didn't learn that well in such a boring environment. I needed to have a more hands-on approach. Which was why I was so good with maps —I could experience what they represented.

Edmund seemed a bit happier, which, again, was probably because of Cor's absence. Although he wouldn't be able to give Cor an earful like he wanted, I had a feeling he was more satisfied with him simply not being here. Zach was also in a good mood, but that had more to do with the fact his belly was full than anything else.

All of our moods changed as we got closer to the capitol. I wasn't sure about the others, but I had a sense of dread wash over me. What if the council didn't want to go to war against Jonathan? What if we had our hopes pulled out from under us all over again? What if they took one look at us and decided that it wasn't worth it?

But I couldn't let such fears stop me—I had to at least try. Otherwise, I would never know the answer.

The four of us entered the capitol. Part of me felt as if guards would come rushing from all sides and arrested us, but that wasn't the case. Instead, Riazusryz greeted us with open arms. It was a strange experience that I don't think any of us had experienced.

"Thank you for coming," Riazusryz said, nodding.

"Thank you for listening to us and for our hotel rooms. You have no idea how great a hot shower felt after everything we have been through," Zach commented. "And the buffet was to die for."

"By how bad you all smelled, I could only imagine. And I am glad you enjoyed the food. Now please come this way." Riazusryz led us down the corridor.

Part of me felt like this was a trap—that nothing could ever be easy and that someone was going to betray us or even try to kill us. We had faced challenges every step of the way thus far—could things finally go smoothly? Or was Riazusryz going to betray our trust just like everyone else had. Just like Jonathan had.

"Weren't there five of you?" Riazusryz asked over his shoulder. "What happened to the blond haired one?"

I answered, "He ended up going after Gabe—the half-Sirian that was with Jonathan."

Riazusryz let out a sigh. "It was clear that boy didn't want to be there, but I wasn't sure—at least, not until Jonathan held a gun to him. I wish I could have done something, but it wasn't the time or place to confront Jonathan. I hope your friend is able to save him."

I nodded. "We all agree."

Riazusryz opened the door, and a group of Lyrans were waiting for us. I gulped. They all could easily overtake us if they wanted. We wouldn't stand a chance. I knew I shouldn't be so paranoid as they wanted to help us, but after everything we had gone through, I couldn't help it.

"Please take a seat." Riazusryz gestured to the large table where there were plenty of seats left.

We all took our seats, Claude and my brother sitting next to me. Zach sat next to Edmund.

"Now let us get started," Riazusryz began as he sat at the head of the table. "The council would like to hear that tale you told me earlier, but in more detail. Please tell them what you told me, starting from the beginning."

Zach and I glanced at each other. I decided to start and told the tale we had now told to leaders in multiple nations. Zach intervened and added to the story when he felt I left something out. We, of course, left out what happened in the mountains and said that we found Claude and Edmund on the road here. It wasn't a complete lie—there had been a road involved. Well, one snowy path.

After the two of us finished our story, the Lyrans all glanced at one another.

"This has gone on too long," one of the Lyrans with a large mane and stripes said. "That family must be stopped."

"But how," another Lyran with white fur asked. "Their family owns most of the Human Zone and has their fingers in a lot of businesses throughout all the zones. We could meet resistance on our own soil if we declare war against him."

"But if we don't do anything, he will attack our zone. We can't let that happen—we must act now," the first Lyran said.

"There could be civil war within our own zone!"

"Enough!" Riazusryz exclaimed. "Settle down. Now I agree there is the threat of our own citizens turning their backs on our nation, but that threat is much lower than Jonathan trying to take action against us. That was clear in his meeting today. He has even taken his own son as hostage to try to get these four to stop from telling us what monstrosities have happened. We must act now. I am putting it to a vote: Who here agrees to declare war against Jonathan Pickett?"

Seven of the nine Lyrans raised their hands.

Riazusryz nodded. "It is settled. Now first things first—we need to find allies in this war. I declare we stop the war effort against the Silurians and settle things with them. We should be able to come up with a treaty after telling them what happened and how it was Byron who was the one who got their leader killed and set them up. The Sirians will not listen to us—not to mention it sounds like Jonathan is going to use his son to get them in his favor. I have been gathering some of the companies that Jonathan owns, and they would be more than willing."

"Will that still be enough warriors to take out Byron?" the white-furred Lyran asked.

"I believe there are plenty of humans who, when they hear you are going to war with Jonathan, they will come with their support," I said.

They all stared at me. "How do you know that?" Riazusryz asked. "Why would they not have loyalty to him?"

I shrugged. "We can't be the only ones who got screwed over by Jonathan. I know if I heard on the radio that there was war, I would do whatever I could to make sure he paid for what he did."

Riazusryz laughed. "That is true—that family has upset a lot of people, especially businesses. Perhaps we should reach out and ask them to give us our support. Zekrunmirr, you are in charge of reaching out to those contacts. Any extra hands will help. I will contact the new leader of the Silurians. Macaamchox, you will ready our forces. We will attack by the week's end."

Everyone at the table nodded. Claude squeezed my hand.

We did it. We'd gotten someone to declare war against Jonathan, and we would stop at nothing until he was six feet under.

CHAPTER XXVI

Zach

We had done it—we found someone to side with us in the war against Jonathan.

But whether we would succeed was another matter. I didn't know if Riazusryz was going to be capable of rallying enough troops to defeat Jonathan and the Human Zone. I felt for the humans that would fight on his side—especially the ones that worked in the companies he had bought from under Jonathan's nose. I had a feeling that

Riazusryz treated them better than Jonathan or Byron ever did. As for the rest of the humans, well, I hoped they could convince them to side with us. It wasn't their fault they were on the wrong side of this war. They didn't know the truth—they didn't know about all the atrocities that Jonathan committed. They just thought he was trying to bring good to this world—or at least their world.

By the sounds of it, there were plenty of humans that would side with the Lyrans due to things Jonathan or Byron did to them in the past. I couldn't only imagine how many enemies they had made over the years, thinking they were invincible and that no one could stop them. They didn't realize that although maybe their enemies couldn't stop them single-handedly, if they banded together, then they were a force to be reckoned with.

The meeting with the council was a lot shorter than I expected, although I had a feeling we only saw the tail end of it—no pun intended. The suns were beginning to set and tomorrow we would find out if Riazusryz was able to get more of the troops.

As we made our way down the street, I wondered how successful Cor was currently for finding Gabe. I hoped Gabe was safe, but Ellie was right—we needed to stop this war once and for all. And the only way to do that was to stay here and help the Lyrans. If we acted rash, Jonathan might also do something rash, and it would all be for nothing. Cor might cause all of that, but at least we would be here to clean up his mess.

I glanced over to Ellie, who was holding Claude's hand. They were cute together, I had to admit. I wondered if they would run off together after this was all said and done. I didn't want things to change between me and Ellie—we had been by each other's side constantly for three years, and even before that as teens and kids—but I also wanted her to be happy. If being with Claude made her happy, then I needed to suck it up and find my own way in life. Besides, who knew what the future held.

We made it back to our hotel and all went into Ellie and Claude's room. Ellie had gotten some clothes she felt more comfortable in— shirt and pants—and quickly changed into them. I couldn't blame her for not wanting to wear a dress as they seemed uncomfortable and fighting in them would be hard. Ellie and I had learned we had to always be on our guard, especially in bars where she liked to pick a fight with someone.

"Do you think Jonathan will be able to talk the Sirians into helping them?" Edmund asked.

Ellie shook her head. "Honestly, I don't think that is possible. The Sirians don't like to get involved with any other zone. Even if he is able to convince them to help, it will take a while for them to come to an agreement."

"Do you think he will kill Gabe to win them over?" I asked as my chest tightened.

Ellie shrugged. "I really don't know. That would be one way to do it, and we know he is capable of such things. He already tried to kill Gabe after all. But maybe he will keep him alive and convince the Sirians that it was all Byron and try to get Gabe to rule."

"Gabe wouldn't do as his father says, would he? He wouldn't be the best puppet for Jonathan," I commented.

"Not without a bargaining chip, no. But Gabe has a sister, and he could easily threaten her to get Gabe to do what he wants," Ellie added.

That sadly seemed likely. Maybe he would keep Gabe alive, knowing he had some leverage in that way. Gabe's sister was not his daughter, so he would need someone with some kind of connection to get things to move a little smoother. Perhaps he would be capable of taking over the Sirian Zone, but that would all still take some time, which I doubt he had.

"The Lyrans are going to contact the Silurians and strike a deal. I don't believe the Silurians will hesitate with that deal—especially with everything that has happened. The only issue will be having to travel across Mu to negotiate the treaties in person. Jonathan will get to the Sirian Zone much quicker than us. He could use that time to gain control, at least in a worst-case scenario," Ellie explained.

"With the Sirian Zone," Claude began, "would he be able to outnumber the Lyrans and the Silurians?"

Ellie shrugged. "I don't know, but I assume so. There are a lot of humans. But Riazusryz said there were a lot of humans who had money and power that had been screwed over by Byron and Jonathan. Odds are, depending on if they have control over towns or not, they could side with us as well. We'll just have to wait for them."

That was all out of our wheelhouse. Although the two of us were bounty hunters, we had never fought in a battle like this. There seemed to be many factors at play—factors that we never thought about. But we would help in whatever way we could, which would probably include being on the front lines, shooting guns, and hoping for the best.

I didn't want to kill, but I also didn't want Jonathan to win this battle. If we didn't stop him here, he would have his way and take control of all of Mu. We couldn't let that happen.

A couple of days passed as we waited for news from the Silurian Zone. Riazusryz kept us updated each day, but it was slow. It took days to travel that far, and while they could communicate using a telephone, they wanted embassies to discuss details.

Other Lyran officials were contacting the humans that could potentially help us, but we hadn't heard anything about how that was going either. It was all a waiting game.

Meanwhile, Jonathan could already be in the Sirian Zone setting up what he needed to do, not to mention he would be more difficult to reach to destroy. None of this felt as if it were going to go our way, and as we wandered the streets of Kiron, more scenarios of how this would all go wrong played in my head.

Most of the day, we readied our weapons and practiced fighting. I wasn't prepared to kill for this war, but I also wasn't going to let myself die. We had to save this planet—we had to save all the races even if they didn't try to save ours.

Then, maybe after all this was over, we could notify the Kausians and rebuild our home.

As we were talking about what to get for dinner, one of Riazusryz's assistants came to our hotel room. He was a spotted Lyran with short fur.

"Riazusryz would like to invite you to dinner. Please be at his residence in an hour." With that, she left us.

"That was… ominous," Claude commented.

Ellie bit at her nail. "I wonder if that means they heard back from the Silurians or the humans who hate Jonathan."

I stood and stretched. "Well, only one way to find out."

We reached Riazusryz's residence right on time.

There were multiple Lyrans arriving as well—the ones that had been at the council meeting days earlier. My heart rate began to quicken. Was this it? Were we officially declaring war? Had they received their responses?

The four of us made our way inside and took a seat. Drinks were brought out to us along with an appetizer. I did my best not to dive in but wait for others to start eating before I took a bite.

Riazusryz was seated at the head of the table and waited for everyone to get settled before speaking. As we all took our seat, he stood up.

"I have brought you all here today to discuss some good news. The Silurians have agreed to our terms and are moving their forces toward the Human Zone. Not only this, but we have already begun negotiations with seven companies within the Human Zone that are cutting ties with Jonathan's war effort and are sending us their men and resources. By the end of the day tomorrow, we will have declared war against Jonathan and anyone who stands with him."

Everyone at the table applauded, including the four of us.

War would begin, and we were going to be

smack dab in the middle of it.

CHAPTER XXVII

Cor

That soldier was right—Jonathan was heading toward Tattingborough. I was able to find a horse—or rather steal a horse—and make my way to the city to find him surrounded by his soldiers.

There was no way I was going to be able to get past them to get to Jonathan. If I killed him now, perhaps I could stop this war from happening. Or, perhaps, I would just be killed in the process, and his people would still declare war. Or my attempt would cause him to harm Gabe. I had no idea what would happen, which made me hesitate for what I wanted to do next.

Perhaps Ellie was right—focusing on the war rather than Gabe was the strongest strategy.

But I had to save him—I couldn't leave him behind. Not again. I had done wrong by Ellie and him countless times. I had to make it right. I had to do right by him.

Otherwise I would be utterly alone.

I shouldn't have thought like that, but the fact Ellie had moved on with someone I had loathed to be around as a teen frustrated me. I couldn't blame her, though, as she deserved happiness. I just didn't want the guy who kept trying to steal my girl to win in the end. And I didn't want to see that smug look on Edmund's face—that is, if I survived this.

I followed Jonathan around for a bit, careful to make sure no one noticed me lingering. I kept my eyes out for any sign of Gabe, but I saw no signs of him. I had no idea where he was or whether he was alive. The odds were that he was locked away somewhere in Jonathan's apartment, but I couldn't know that for a fact.

What if he was dead? What if I was too late? I

had to calm myself down every few minutes as panic kept trying to set in. Then, after a couple of days of following Jonathan, Gabe finally appeared.

He was fine—better than fine. I had expected Jonathan to torture him, but he appeared healthier than he had when I had last seen him. Was Jonathan going to try to use him to get the Sirians to side with him? Was Jonathan really that desperate and thought it would work?

Although Gabe seemed fine, I could tell he was angry and frustrated. He looked at his father with such hatred in his eyes—hatred I had never seen before. Gabe was a pretty relaxed person and didn't let things get to him—so seeing him with Byron and Jonathan had been an experience. I didn't know he had it in him, but it was always the quiet ones that had the darkest secrets.

I watched as Gabe hesitated, but it was apparent that whatever his father was going to make him do, he was not okay with it. The odds were he was going to use him to take over the Sirian Zone.

How he was going to do that, I had no idea. But I knew that if I tried anything, Jonathan would end his son's life right then and there. I would have to be careful and try to get to Gabe without Jonathan or his guards noticing. Jonathan was on high alert after everything that happened, and knowing that the Lyran Zone was going to declare war on him, he wasn't letting anyone near him.

Gabe followed Jonathan into a carriage. I got onto my horse and headed after them. After they made a few turns, I knew exactly where they were going—they were going to the docks.

Which meant they weren't wasting any more time and were going to the Sirian Zone.

I cursed under my breath. I wasn't sure how I was going to follow them down there. I was pretty sure that everyone there would shoot me on sight. There would be wanted posters everywhere even with the borders closed—which a whole different problem. I had no way to get down there as there were no public shuttles.

Jonathan probably had his own underwater machine, so it wasn't as if I could catch the ferry after his. No, I would have to transform and swim and pray no one noticed I was a Kausian.

Even though I had good reason to transform, it still felt odd to change my appearance in public. Yes, when I was a prostitute, I would change my appearance, but that was different. I was trying to make my employers' wishes come true, whereas right now I would be breaking the law as a Kausian and using my powers. Not only that, but I would be using them to try to take down someone in power and to trespass closed borders.

Really, I should be afraid of the last two things more than just transforming, but the other zones made sure Kausian grew up afraid of their powers. I knew some people who never transformed their entire lives, even inside the Kausian Zone. I also knew people who would transform a lot, and, well, they were killed. So I had every right the hesitate. Even up in the mountains, none of them seemed to transform.

But it was all or nothing now. I would transform into a Sirian, I would swim down to the zone, and I would do anything to make sure Gabe was fine. I had to—I owed him that much.

CHAPTER XXVIII

Gabe

I did not like this plan, but I had to keep my sister safe, and I knew this would be the only way to do it.

Even if I refused, Jonathan would still get his way. If he killed me, he could get the Sirians to trust him and then he would simply manipulate my sister into doing what he says. I couldn't let her get involved with this—I couldn't let her near this man. If I took over the Sirian Zone, then I could keep her safe. The Lyrans and the others would have to take Jonathan down. It was up to them now. I would just keep him distracted by doing what he says until then.

There was no way I could do anything to my father without there being severe consequences, if not just being killed in the process. He was smarter than me and a lot better at violence. And although I hated him, he was still my father, and I wasn't sure if I could pull the trigger. If I wasn't able to kill the Kausian who killed my mother, how would I be able to kill him?

We made it to Jonathan's shuttle, and I wondered what exactly his plan was. Sure, they might believe him about Byron being the one who assassinated my mother, but that didn't mean they would accept me. I wasn't too worried about it, other than the fact that they might try to kill me on the spot. This wasn't my plan, and it would honestly be better if it failed right away and the Sirians didn't give their forces to Jonathan. But I had a feeling that wasn't going to happen.

Before we left, Jonathan readied the human forces. If the Lyrans attacked, they would be at the ready. They would also await Jonathan's orders after he spoke to the Sirians. If he can get the Sirians to work with him, then he would begin the war against the Lyrans. From what he told me, he would have double the number of soldiers compared to the Lyrans, and it would be easy to conquer them even if they were fierce warriors. Even with just humans, his forces outnumbered them, although there was also the Silurians that they were fighting. I wondered if the Lyrans would team up with them or not.

I tried not to worry about any of that and focused on the fact that Ellie and the others were taking care of that. Ellie would come up with a plan—they all would. They were smart and had survived this long—there was no way Jonathan could win. Not after everything they had been through.

I took a seat in the shuttle, and Jonathan ordered the driver to head down to the Sirian Zone. Before the driver could protest, as the Sirian Zone border was closed, my father demanded he start the shuttle that instant and get down there. The driver didn't argue, the vehicle started up, and we made our way to the Sirian Zone.

Glancing out the glass, I thought about how I didn't believe I would ever see my home again, especially so soon. I knew I wanted to see my sister and make sure she remembered that it wasn't me that killed our mother but some impostor. I wanted to see her again, and I had feared earlier I would never see her.

But I didn't want to be here under these circumstances.

No. I wanted more than anything to go back to land and run away. I didn't want to bring destruction to my home—I didn't want to bring war. But it was inevitable whether I was here or not.

Jonathan and Byron made sure of that.

I wondered what Cor was up to and whether I would ever see him again. Part of me felt as if he were close, but I knew that wasn't true. He had no reason to go after me. He would be risking his life, and that was just something Cor wouldn't do. No, he would help Ellie and the others try to take down Jonathan. I was a lost cause at this point. There was no way anyone could help me out of this position—not without completely destroying Jonathan, and to be honest, that didn't see possible. He was too evil.

"What are you thinking about, my son?" Jonathan asked as we were well into the sea.

I turned to him. "Nothing that concerns you."

"Are you thinking about the Kausian you love oh so much?"

I glared at him, and he chuckled. "I figured as much. You know Cor is bad news, don't you? And his heart belongs to someone else. You two would have never worked out. I saw the way he looks at Elvira—you have nothing on her. He was going to leave you in the end—I am saving you the trouble."

I didn't respond, because it wouldn't matter. I knew deep down he was wrong, and Cor did love me, but part of me wondered the same. Was Cor going to leave me for Ellie? Would I be alone in the end?

It was the last thing I should be worrying if I were honest, and yet here I was, thinking about Cor and not about the fate of the entire world. I was pathetic. I shouldn't let my father manipulate me— I should be focusing on how I was going to use his own plan against him.

The problem was, there were always a few guards around us. I couldn't take them all out, and they were all loyal to Jonathan. As to why, I wasn't sure. Perhaps money really did make the world go round, or perhaps they had the same beliefs as

Jonathan. Either way, they weren't going to see reason.

A couple of hours passed, and we finally reached the Sirian Zone. My whole body was shaking as I feared about what would happen next. Were they going to kill me on the spot? Did my sister believe the lies that I had killed our mother? Or did she remember the truth?

As we approached, a figure was waiting at the dock. My father greeted him.

"Laguna, it is good to see you! I see that you received my message."

The Sirian that had been waiting for us was Laguna, one of my mother's councilmen. This was not a good sign. Perhaps my father had more pull than I realized. I had believed they all hated him and loved Byron—at least, that how it always seemed to me.

"That I did, and I am here to hear what you want to say and to provide safe passage through the city." He eyed me, and I gulped.

Had the seeds already been sown by Jonathan? Was I mistaken when I thought my people would not allow me to rule? Did Jonathan already have connections here, and I was a piece he needed to retrieve?

"That is great to hear. Shall we?" Jonathan gestured in front of him.

Laguna led us to the tram that would take us to the palace. Luckily there weren't many people, but those who were around stared at me, gasping in horror. They appeared like they wanted to say something until they saw Laguna was with us. They more than likely didn't know the truth—Laguna probably didn't tell them about Jonathan or anything else that was going to happen.

We made our way to the palace, and I worried about seeing my sister. I wondered if she would greet me with happiness or blame me for everything. I didn't know if I could handle her seeing me as a monster, but I understood her pain all too well.

"Well, son, how does it feel to be home?"

I didn't answer him but simply stared out at the city. This place never truly felt like home or, at least, what I imagined home to feel like. The only time I felt as if I was at home was when I was with the people that accepted me, like Cor did. Like all of them did.

And Jonathan took that away from me. He took

everything away from me.

We arrived to the palace, and Laguna ushered us to a room full of Sirian officials. I could feel the color from my face drain. What was this about?

Jonathan opened his arms. "Gentleman! I am glad you could make it. If you would be so kind, please inform my son about the war efforts we have already established."

CHAPTER XXIX

Ellie

We awoke to a siren.

The ground was shaking all around us. My ears were ringing from the sound of the siren and the sound of explosions. My entire body felt frozen. I knew this sound—I knew this feeling. Bombs were going off outside. War had started.

Claude shook me, and I snapped out of it. I cursed under my breath for letting it get to me. I should have expected Jonathan to play a dirty trick like this—to bomb an innocent town instead of fight army against army. He wanted panic—he wanted chaos. Just like they did with Kaus. This was all part of his plan.

Grabbing me by the arm, Claude pulled me out of the bed as we grabbed our weapons and hurried out of the hotel. The ground shook. Another bomb had been catapulted into the town.

"Fuck!" I yelled as I hurried after him into the hallway. The ground shook and I rammed into the wall. I glanced at Edmund and Zach's rooms—the doors were open which meant they had already headed outside. I must have been a little hard to wake for Claude, or I was frozen longer than I realized.

Zach and Edmund weren't to far ahead of us when we made down the emergency exit. Screams echoed through the streets as people tried to find their loved ones and head to a safe place. There must have been shelters somewhere for them—every town had them. Every town didn't trust other nations.

Which was probably how some of the Kausians survived.

"What should we do?" Zach yelled over the

alarm.

I watched as a piece of metal shot through the sky. Another bomb. How many did they have?

"Take cover!" I yelled as it hit a building nearby. Sure enough, the building exploded—pieces of brick going every direction. More screams filled the area.

"We have to hurry," Edmund said. "Before the entire area is flattened."

None of us said anything, as we knew we were all thinking the same thing—we had been through this before, and we knew what to do.

"The attack is coming from that direction." I pointed. "Let's go!"

"You can't be serious," Zach exclaimed. "You think we should run toward it?"

"We have to stop them," I said. "We can't let what happened on Kaus happen here."

I knew Zach wanted to say that there was no possible way that we could stop them, but he didn't say anything. We kept forward toward where the cannons were firing the bombs. I noticed that soldiers were also headed that way.

Good, I thought. We were not alone.

Claude and Edmund followed us as well,

knowing that the only way to stop this was to kill the men behind the guns. We hurried after the Lyran soldiers, hoping they had pinpointed where the bombs were coming from better than we could.

Sure enough, they had. And Jonathan had sent more than just a couple of men. There was a whole troop lying in wait. They began firing.

"Get down!" I screamed as I pulled Claude down with me as he was the closest. Both he and I and the others took cover as the sound of machine guns filled the air. The air ruffled above us as the bullets flew past and hit the Lyran soldiers that had been behind us.

There was a metallic smell in the air. Blood stained the grass. I wanted to help them and get them to a hospital, but we had to move forward— we had to save this land before it was too late.

Because if the Lyran Zone went down, so would the rest of Mu.

I pulled out my gun and began shooting. I heard one of the humans cry out. Direct hit.

Thank goodness Riazusryz gave us guns and real bullets. Not many would trust the likes of us. And they were expensive, but perhaps to a governor preparing for war they weren't. And he knew we needed us—we had survived this long after all.

I shot another two men, and they hit the ground and began to roll toward us. I quickly grabbed their guns and tossed one to Claude.

"Cover me," I said as I glanced over to see how many more men there were. There was at least a dozen that I could see—probably more hidden in the dark. This was not going to be easy.

"Ellie…," Zach said in a huff, but it was too late —I was already up and running toward the group of men. I heard Claude cock the machine gun and start firing it in the direction that the men were. I could trust him to be there for me—that much I knew.

I could tell Zach was upset that I had run off to be in the middle of a fight yet again. He worried about me, and I appreciated that, but I could take care of myself. As long as they watched my back and covered for me, of course.

The men noticed me coming, and at first they appeared flustered since I was not a Lyran, but then they realized I was not their backup, and I meant business. The first man got ready to fire, but I shot him first. He hit the ground, and many of the other soldiers were turning their aim at me. I was about to be outnumbered.

Shots were fired from behind me, and I knew my friends had my back. Another three went down, and I shot the man closest to me. Five down, another seven to go. That I could see, at least.

Another one of the men came running toward me as they pulled out their gun. I watched as they fell to the ground. Claude stepped up next to me.

"You are pretty reckless, you know that?" Claude commented.

I smiled. "Just a bit, but I had it."

"Sure you did. But we have a few more to take out."

I sighed. "I noticed. It's going to be a long night."

"First things first, we need to take out the guy controlling the cannon," Claude commented.

"You read my mind."

Claude and I made our way to the cannon that was still firing bombs at the city. Edmund and Zach covered our back.

Whatever this was, Jonathan wasn't playing fair. To attack a town at night before war was officially declared was playing dirty. Well, two could play that game. He forgot that some of the best gunmen were here. I, of course, meant Zach and me.

Claude took down two more people. Perhaps he was a better gunman than I thought. Maybe he could have won the shooting competition where we won the horses. Although, that had more to do with luck than it had to do with skill.

With Zach and Edmund behind us, and the rest of the Lyran squad now appearing and making stride against the human soldiers, we were able to take out the men manning the cannon. I glanced around at the bodies. They weren't all humans—there were Sirians in the mix.

This was not a good sign.

CHAPTER XXX

Zach

The people in the town began to search through the rubble to see what was left and searched for those who survived—or didn't. Those who needed immediate care were rushed to the hospital, which was luckily not damaged in the attack, and everyone who could lent a helping hand.

The leaders of the Lyran Zone met together in the capitol building, which was one of the few buildings that were still standing. The four of us went with, as Riazusryz held us in high esteem, for whatever reason—I still wasn't sure.

We sat at the table as Riazusryz vented. He slammed his fists on the table.

"How dare he attack a town like this! That is not how a war between zones is performed!"

I wanted to comment that was how the Silurians attacked Kaus, but I held my tongue as did the others.

"We have to retaliate!" he went on. "We must find Jonathan and take him out at once!"

"Sir," of the Lyrans said. "There have been reports that some of the men who were involved in the attack were Sirians, and we have word he and his son are in the Sirian Zone. They are making a treaty as we speak."

Riazusryz rubbed his eyes. "This is the worst-case scenario. Not only have they committed war crimes against us, weakening our forces, but they have also gained forces."

Ellie raised her hand. "Sir, if I may be so bold as to speak."

He waved her on. "Go ahead."

Ellie glanced at us, then said, "Send the four of us to the Sirian Zone. We can sneak in by transforming into Sirians. We can take Jonathan out that way. If he is, in fact, using Gabe, he is going to put him in a position of power as his son. Once Jonathan is dead, as his son, Gabe can call off this war."

I wasn't sure if that plan would work, but I agreed with her—it was worth a shot. It wasn't as if we would have to worry about a war starting when it already had. I glanced at Claude and Edmund who didn't seem opposed either. They wanted this done and over with.

Ellie went on. "I know it's a long shot, but it might be the only way to stop him. Even if they don't accept Gabe, we'll get rid of one of our main problems."

Riazusryz considered this. "You would be risking your life not only by trying to assassinate Jonathan, but if you are caught transformed into another species, you will be sentenced to death."

Ellie shrugged. "We just won't get caught."

Easy for her to say—we had been caught many times; we were just faster than our assailants.

Riazusryz took a deep breath and let it out slowly. "Fine, do it."

We gathered some of the things that survived in the hotel last night and prepared right away for our journey. Riazusryz was providing two extra horses and readying Kevin and Charlotte as we put together our bags.

"You two don't have to come with us," Ellie told Claude and Edmund. "Zach and I can handle this. This isn't your fight."

Edmund shook his head. "We made our decision when we left the mountains with you. We want to see this war end once and for all. Then perhaps we can finally go home."

Claude nodded. "He's right—we aren't leaving you, not after all this time."

Ellie smiled and glanced away. "Thank you both. I just hope we can succeed."

Because otherwise we will be killed. None of us said that, but we were all thinking it.

We finished gathering our things and headed out on our horses. I was happy to be with Charlotte again, but part of my mind wondered once we got there if we would ever see them again. We might not make it out alive.

We traveled for a day to the closest port that led down to the Sirian Zone. Riazusryz gave us money to board the horses, and we did just that. Ellie and I took a moment with our horses, afraid of what was to come. As we walked out of the stables, Ellie patted my back.

"We will make it out alive, and they will be there waiting."

I nodded. "Right. We have to survive, just for them."

"Exactly. Now stop your worrying and focus on the task at hand."

"Do you really think we will be successful? Or that it will make a difference?" I asked. "I mean, we were originally afraid to kill him because that would make him a martyr."

Ellie looked down at her feet. "I think it doesn't matter anymore. I think taking him out will stop a lot of the problems, but you are right—he has put a lot of the pieces in motion already. I am just hoping that Gabe can step up and take his place. If he is going through all this trouble to set up Gabe as a pawn now, he must need him for something. And perhaps he can then take his father's place and stop

this war."
  "Let's hope you are right."

CHAPTER XXXI

Cor

I was able to trick the guards into letting me into the city. I kept my eyes down, and they didn't think twice as they let me through the gates. It wasn't as if Kausians were typically a threat. At least, not anymore.

The next part would be even more difficult. I knew Gabe would be taken to the palace, which was a bit more guarded, and they would be checking people more closely. Luckily, I knew the layout of the palace and wouldn't be completely lost if I managed to sneak inside.

This was one of those moments where I missed Ellie. She was good at figuring out how to get in and out of places without anyone knowing. There were other instances where I missed Ellie, but at this moment, I needed her brains.

I would have to stake out the area to start. Perhaps Jonathan or Gabe would leave sometime soon, and I could grab him then. Or perhaps I could watch and wait for some shift of workers, like cleaners or something. I could knock one out and take their clothes. Yeah, that would work. It had to.

I got close enough to the palace where I could keep an eye on what was happening but was far enough where no one really took notice of me. I had to keep a distance from Sirians or else they might notice my eye color, and everything would be for naught.

Waiting for a few hours, I noticed the people did not go in or out of the palace that often, which was going to be trouble. Did the workers simply live in the palace? Or had I not waited long enough?

As my attention was on the palace, I didn't notice figures approach from behind me. Before I could react, one grabbed me and threw me back.

"Oof!" I slammed down on the ground. The figure straddled me and held a knife to my throat. Before they sliced my throat open, the figure sighed.

"Cor? Seriously? I almost killed you."

It was Ellie. I looked up to find her also transformed into a Sirian. Behind her were the others.

"What are you all doing here?" I asked as Ellie got off me.

"The same as you—saving Gabe. Well," she went on. "Killing Jonathan and hoping Gabe can take over his empire, or whatever you want to call it."

I couldn't believe it. "There is no way Gabe will take over all of that."

"Well, too bad. He has to try. We can't do this without him."

I had been with Gabe for a couple of years now, and if there was one thing I knew for certain was that he was not a person who would do good in a position of authority. He was too much of a pushover, which was exactly why he was in the position he was in now. His father was more than likely using his sister to get Gabe to do what he wanted. He wasn't a fighter—he wasn't someone who could come up with a cunning plan—he just went with the flow and hoped for the best.

"I don't think it will work, but either way we have to get in there. Have any ideas?"

"Oh, Cor. I always have a plan."

I grinned. That was the Ellie I knew.

Sure enough, Ellie did have a plan. She knew when the changing of the guards would be, and we were able to knock out five of the guards and take their clothing. We stepped inside without anyone noticing.

Now the question was where was Gabe? There were many, many levels to this place—it would take a long while to search all the rooms.

"What do you think," I asked Ellie. "Where is he?"

"Well," she began. "When I checked the maps last time we were here, there was a level with meeting rooms which could be one place he is. The other place would be either in his room, if they repaired it, with his sister, or wherever they might place Jonathan."

"Maybe the queen's quarters?" I commented. "Jonathan is a sicko and might stay in there."

Ellie nodded. "That's a good thought. It's still midday though, so I'm not sure if Jonathan would be in there. Our best bet would be to grab Gabe's sister and go from there. We can keep her safe so Gabe won't be afraid of his father any longer."

"Good idea. Let's go."

Ellie led us up the stairs. I hated these stairs so much. We had gone up and down them so many times now—I wished to never see them again.

Once we were ten flights up, Ellie entered the corridor. We kept an eye out for anyone who seemed out of place. As we got closer to Gabe's sister's room, we noticed more guards. Luckily, we were dressed the same as they were, so they didn't question why we were there.

"Finally," one of them said. "We have been waiting to be dismissed."

Apparently the guards we had knocked out were supposed to come here. That worked out perfectly for us.

"Sorry about that. We are here now," I said.

They didn't wait another moment and headed down the corridor. I let go of the breath I had been holding. That was too close. It was clear no one really looked at us in the eyes or questioned when we tried to keep our head down.

"Well, that was lucky," Claude commented. "Now what?"

"We grab Gabe's sister and then go find him," Ellie answered as she pushed the button to open the door.

Sure enough, a young Sirian was inside. She was clutching a whale plush, her eyes full of tears. Ellie knelt down as she transformed into her normal look.

"Hello, Kishiko. Do you remember me?"

Kishiko looked at her. "You… you are one of my brother's friends."

Ellie nodded. "That's right. And we're here to help you and your brother. Will you come with us?"

Kishiko nodded. "Yes. And I know where they are."

"You do?" I asked. I honestly didn't expect her to know what was going on.

"Yes, they are in my mama's room. Gabe was yelling at his father, and they took me away after that man threatened me."

So we were right—Jonathan was using her as leverage.

Ellie picked her up. "Then let's go. We have no time to waste. But just so you know, I am going to transform into a Sirian, and you have to act like I am not a Kausian, okay?"

She nodded. "Okay."

With the sister, we headed up more flights of stairs toward where the queen used to sleep. My heart rate quickened. What were we going to do once we got there? Were we just going to shoot Jonathan? It couldn't be that easy, could it?

There were a handful of human guards at the door. I heard Ellie whisper something in Kishiko's ear, and she shut her eye tight. Ellie nodded toward the rest of us as she pulled out her gun.

I guess we were just going to shoot all the guards. That would have been good to know beforehand.

The four of us pulled out our guns and shot the men standing there. They weren't expecting such an attack and didn't have time to defend themselves. They all hit the ground with a thud.

Pressing the button, the door slid open, and all of us stopped in our tracks at what we saw.

Gabe standing above his father with a gun in his hand.

CHAPTER XXXII

Gabe

The world was spinning around me.

What had happened? One moment we were standing here talking. Arguing. And then all I saw was red. Next thing I knew, there was a gun in my hand and my father was on the ground, dead.

Then it hit me. I had killed my father. My own flesh and blood.

I collapsed on the ground, hyperventilating. There was no way that just happened. I couldn't have killed him. This was some trick.

But it wasn't. He was dead. He told me he was going to hurt my sister, and when we heard the chaos outside, I took that second to grab his gun and shoot him.

I felt someone wrap their arms around me and squeeze me. Who was in here? What was going on? I tried to focus, but everything was swirling.

"Breathe, Gabe. It's okay. We are here."

It was Cor. How did he find me? How was he able to get down here? And who did he mean by we?

My eyes began to focus, and I realized I wasn't alone. Ellie, Claude, and Edmund were here as well. And my sister.

"Kishiko," I exclaimed. "You are okay."

Ellie set her down, and she ran over to me and wrapped her small arms around me. "Big brother, you are okay."

But I wasn't okay. I had killed my father in cold blood.

I was shaking now. I knew my father hated me—I knew I was just a part of his scheme—but he was still my father, and I had let my anger take control of me and killed him. I was no different than he was.

"Gabe." Ellie knelt beside me. "I know you just did something terrible and are dealing with that mentally and emotionally, but you have to go and talk to the Sirian council and tell them to call off the war against the Lyrans. Jonathan was committing war crimes and attacking defenseless villages. Who knows what other orders he gave. You have to stop it."

I shook my head. "No, I can't. They will not listen to me. All this is pointless. The war is going to go on, and it will have been all my fault."

Ellie grabbed my cheeks and forced me to look at her. "No. You are going to go in there and you are going to use your father's charisma and confidence to get them to stop. You hear me? You have what it takes—just act like him but actually have a heart. You can do this—I know you can."

I stared at her. Why did she have so much faith in me? I couldn't do that—I couldn't act like my father and get them to side with me. That would be impossible.

My sister's arms tightened around me. "I don't want there to be war, big brother. She's right, you have to stop it."

I turned my attention down to her. She was just a child, but she was already more confident than I was. Why did I have such a problem with confidence? Why couldn't I be more like the others?

"Gabe," Cor began. "I know you are afraid, but she is right—you have to do this. It is hard doing the right thing, believe me. But if you don't go in there and stop this, you will regret it for the rest of your life. You are the only one who can stop this war. Your father made you a pawn in all this, and it is time to change that. You can now be the one in control if you can prove you are strong enough."

He was right. I had to be strong, not only for myself but for all of them. I stood up. "Fine. Let's go."

I called upon the council that my father had set up here. It was full of Sirians and the humans he and Byron had wrapped around his finger. Now it was my turn. I had always been the scared little boy hiding in the corner, but not this time. I wouldn't let them push me around. I had to live up to my legacy and take control.

Because I was the only one who could.

"What is the meaning of this?" exclaimed the Sirian councilman that had been working with my father. "Where is Jonathan?"

"Dead," I stated. "And as his rightful heir, I am taking his place."

He let out a laugh. "There is no way we are taking orders from a weakling like you."

"You will. I am the rightful heir to Jonathan's empire, and I am the rightful heir to the Sirian Zone. You yourself made a motion to make me king. I will not have you question my authority!"

The Sirian was taken aback, and to be honest, so was I. I wasn't used to this voice. Perhaps the others were right—perhaps I could be a leader.

Ellie stepped forward. "And if any of you have a problem with that, you will speak to us."

They were back in their Kausian form—they didn't want to get into trouble. They were in stolen guard uniforms, though. That would be a bit easier to explain, at least.

"Right," I said. "And first things first—call off the troops and declare a truce. We will be forming a peace treaty with both the Lyrans and the Silurians."

"You can't be serious—that is not what your

father wanted!"

"I do not care! I am in charge now! Do as I say, or I will find someone else for your position."

The Sirian glared at me for a moment and then turned to the others. "Do as he says. We will call a truce."

I smiled. "Thank you. Now." I took a seat at the head of the table. "Let us begin our reformations."

CHAPTER XXXIII

Ellie

Weeks had passed since Gabe killed his father. As he promised, peace treaties had been signed between all the zones, and, for once, there was peace. Or, at least, there was peace at the moment. I had doubts that all Jonathan's underlings had actually accepted Gabe as their new ruler and might try to overthrow him, but that would a problem for the future to face. Right now, we had to focus on the good things.

Claude and Edmund had gone up to the Kausians in the mountains and told them what had happened. After many elders meetings, and after signed treaties by other zones, the Kausians decided to move back where Kaus once stood. All the nations, as promised in the treaty, would send whatever support we needed to rebuild the town for the better. The technology would be greater than it had been when we were growing up, and until we could get areas for plants to grow, they would also send us food. The ground seemed promising, though, and vegetation was already growing back.

I finished painting the last shingle of the house Claude and I were working on. It was white and had enough room for us, my brother, and Zach for the time being. We also had some farmland that Zach and Claude were beginning to prep the soil for. We would grow some vegetables and fruits that we could sell in town and make a living. It would be a quiet life, but after everything that had happened, I was ready for that.

"Well, looks perfect to me!" Zach said as he finished up the dark blue trim.

I nodded. "It does. I have always wanted a house with these colors, if I am honest."

"And it is everything you deserve," I heard a voice say behind me. It was Cor.

My eyes widened. "What are you doing here? You know if any of the Kausians see you, they will imprison you, if not kill you."

He shrugged. "I know, but I wanted to say goodbye."

We stood there silently for a moment, when Zach finally coughed.

"I think Claude and Edmund need some help. I should go help them." With that, Zach left us standing there.

I turned back to Cor. "So…"

He scratched the back of his head. "Yeah…"

I traced my boot in the dirt. "Are you moving to the Sirian Zone?"

He nodded. "Yeah, Gabe needs to be kept safe. There are a lot of people out there that want his head."

"I bet."

More silence.

"Ellie… I just… I want to say I'm sorry. For everything."

I nodded. "I know."

"I wish this world had been better to us."

"Me too."

Cor scratched the back of his head as he glanced out to the field. "You deserve Claude. He will treat you right."

"He does," I said.

"Do you love him?"

I nodded. "I do. I can rely on him. He cares about me and won't leave me behind."

"Good. You deserve someone like that."

I also glanced out at the field. "And you deserve Gabe. He brings something out of you that I never could."

More silence. A breeze caused hair to fly in my face. I tried move it back behind my ear, but I failed miserably.

Cor chuckled as he helped me. "You are so adorable, Ellie. I will miss you."

"We will see each other again; I have no doubt about that."

He nodded. "Right." He dropped his arm. "Well, I guess, see you around then."

I grabbed his arm and pulled him in for one last kiss. I caught him by surprise, and he laughed as he moved away.

"You always seem to catch me off my guard,

Ellie."

I waved at him as he stepped away. "See you around, Cor."

Acknowledgements

I want to say thank you to everyone who made this possible. First off, my husband who "gets the pleasure" of reading all my stories multiple times and has always stayed by my side and pushed me forward.

Also, my parents and family who have supported me since the beginning. To all my friends who get to put up with me talking about my characters, the research I find, and just getting asked the most random questions. Special thank you to my writing group and writing instructors/mentors who have always supported me and believed in me.

A special thanks to my editors at Victory Editing, the artist for this cover WHO DID A FANTASTIC JOB, Mona Finden, and a thanks to Biserka Designs for formatting and adding the title.

Lastly, thank you to my readers for supporting me by buying my books. I wouldn't be here without you!

Dani Hoots is a young adult sci-fi and fantasy author who is inspired by ancient tales. She has a background in anthropology, classical studies, urban planning, herbal science, and sci-fi writing. She enjoys learning about history, astronomy, and plants, and in her spare time she is either watching anime, reading manga and books, playing the bagpipes dueling with her lightsaber, or drawing. Currently she is going back to school for art.

www.DaniHoots.com

Feel free to email her with any questions you might have!

danihootsauthor@gmail.com

www.ingramcontent.com/pod-product-compliance
Lightning Source LLC
Chambersburg PA
CBHW060911210726

48293CB00006B/2052